FATE SUMMONER

THE FIRE HEART CHRONICLES BOOK 5

JULIANA HAYGERT

COPYRIGHT

AUTHOR'S NOTE

I hope you enjoy reading *Fate Summoner*!

Don't forget to sign up for my Newsletter to find out about new releases, cover reveals, giveaways, and more!

If you want to see exclusive teasers, help me decide on covers, read excerpts, talk about books, etc, join my reader group on Facebook: Juliana's Club!

DICTIONARY

Chey – daughter
Chini – son
Daj – mother
Dat – father
Gadjo – non-Romani person
Nais tuke – thank you
Ozi – fire
Phal – brother
Phen – sister
Puri Chey – granddaughter
Puri Chini – grandson
Puri Daj – grandmother
Puri Dat – grandfather
Rom Baro – leader of the enclave
Ruv – wolf/werewolf
Saint Sara-la-Kali – Romani Saint
Sastimos – a greeting
Vurdon – wagon

Yog – fire
Yog Ozi Nas – fire heart fever

1

______

I didn't think I had ever been happier.

About seven months ago, I had been shoved into this heart maiden business, completely lost, confused, and somewhat scared. I had gone through a lot. I had learned about my lineage and my powers, I had found out my mother had never been honest with me, I had gained a father and two half-brothers, I had found love and gotten my heart broken into a million pieces, and I had made many friends and lost quite a few too. From my inner circle, Sloan, Nico, and Ramon were gone. I had met the previous heart maiden, who somehow was still alive and had gone mad; she was now waging war against me and any other tzigane. I had found out being the heart maiden wasn't all rainbows and sunshine —the magic came with a disease called the fire heart fever, and because of it, I was bound to go mad. Once the elder council found out about it, they would kill me. But then someone new walked into my life about two months ago.

Kane.

The same man who swam toward me right now.

Smiling, I pushed against the water, putting some more distance between us.

"Where do you think you're going?" he asked, his voice husky.

Despite the unusually hot March day and the warm water from the waterfall—which I had heated up using my fire magic—a shiver rolled down my spine.

I had never been happier, and I was sure most of it was because of Kane.

"Away from you," I joked. He knew I wouldn't go too far from him. Ever. Not if I could help it.

One corner of his lips curled up.

By Saint Sara-la-Kali, he was gorgeous. How could he not be, with the laser-cut face, the five o'clock shadow over the sharp angles of his jaw and chin, the piercing hazel eyes, and the long dark brown hair, which was combed back now because of the water. He had come to the Lovell enclave because he had felt a pull inside him. He often said it was because of me. He had come for me. I wasn't sure about that, but one thing I had learned in the past seven months was that nothing was impossible. All that mattered was that the master slayer and his special powers had changed my life.

Kane disappeared under the water, and I knew he was coming for me. I spun around and swam to the shore, but he was much faster than me. His arm snaked around my waist and I yelped. When he emerged from under the water, he tightened his grip around me and pulled my back against his hard chest. He splayed his fingers across my midriff, trapping me in his arms, and he leaned his head forward, brushing his lips on my neck.

A moan escaped my lips.

"I won't let you go, Mirella," he whispered, his mouth on

my ear. His warm breath washed over my skin, sending another rippling shiver through my body. "Never."

I spun in his arms and looked into his hazel eyes. "I'm counting on that."

Kane's hand shot up and he gripped the nape of my neck, pulling me to him. His mouth crashed over mine and I melted into him. There was no way I could resist him. I didn't want to resist. Why would I? He was handsome, hot, took care of me, and treated me like an equal.

He teased me by kissing me hard and deep and fast. With a smirk, he broke the kiss and pulled back a few inches.

I blinked at him. What the hell?

Stifling a chuckle, he asked, "Ready for the ceremony tomorrow?"

I groaned. He really had to bring that up now? "I think so."

The truth was—and he knew it—that I really was. The three-day long festival that started tomorrow was a big deal for the tziganes, and the ceremony I had to perform was even bigger. It was supposed to exile winter and welcome spring, which in theory was supposed to make more heart flowers bloom in the area. Since it could only be performed by a heart maiden, none of the tziganes had seen it done before. All they knew about it was what they had learned from books, journals, or word of mouth.

"You'll be okay. I'm sure of it." Kane reached over and brushed a wet strand of my hair back. "You're strong, intelligent, powerful, caring, beautiful."

My brows furrowed. "What does being beautiful have to do with that?"

A lopsided grin took over Kane's lips. "That's just an added bonus. One I like very much."

I shook my head. "You're impossible."

He gestured to himself. "It's part of my package." My eyes scanned his ripped chest. By Saint Sara-la-Kali, I had a hard time keeping my hands to myself when he was shirtless, or even worse, naked. When he purposely drew my attention to his hot, hot body? I was a goner.

Desire pooled low in my belly, and I closed the distance between us. My eyes fixed on his, I used the water to push me up and wound my arms around his neck. Then, I wrapped my legs around his waist, pressing my hips against his.

Kane let out a low hiss. Slowly, his hands snaked around my body.

"You're so full of yourself," I said, my voice low.

His eyes flicked to my mouth. "And you like it."

"You know it." I licked my lower lip, drawing his gaze back to my mouth.

A groan rumbled from his chest and he leaned into me. His lips found mine again, but this time, he took his time. He controlled the kiss, moving his lips slowly against mine, and I enjoyed every second of it, drinking him in as much as I could.

Deepening the kiss, Kane backed us up until my back hit one of the rocks jutting out of the water by the waterfall. He pressed my back against the rock, careful that there weren't any sections that could hurt me, and pushed his body against mine.

A moan rolled past my tongue.

He broke the kiss, but his lips didn't stop working. They slid down my neck, leaving a trail of fire, fire that wasn't related to my magic. I threw my head back, giving him better access, and he licked the hollow of my throat before nipping the soft spot between my neck and shoulder.

"I could eat you up," he whispered.

My stomach tightened with the thought. "Please do."

He pulled back, enough so he could look at me. "Mirella, I l—"

"There you are."

Her voice was like pellets of ice hitting our backs. Kane and I stiffened and submerged half of our chests into the water before turning to the newcomer.

"Hi, Trina," I said, trying to sound normal, and not a bit upset Kane's ex-wife had interrupted us.

Truth be told, I couldn't be mad at her. Despite her history with Kane and how she had betrayed him, Trina had come to our enclave when we called for help, and if it weren't for her expertise in alchemy, a few dozen tziganes would now be dead.

With a deep frown between her brows, Trina stopped a couple of feet from the edge of the water. "I didn't mean to interrupt." Her voice was tight. Usually, she was outgoing and spat whatever came to mind, but there were a few times in the past two months when I was sure she was hurting on the inside, especially when she looked at Kane and me. Was she jealous? Did she regret cheating on him? As far as I knew, their wedding had been arranged when they were kids. They barely knew each other when they got married and they never loved one another. That didn't change the fact that they had spent a couple of years of their lives together—and *I* was jealous of that. "I just ... I had some thoughts and I had to talk to you, Mi."

She was serious, which prompted me to be serious too. "What is it?" I trudged to the edge of the water.

"It has been two months." Trina started pacing along the lake's bank. "Two months without any problems. We haven't been attacked by alchemists, red alchemists, or revenants. Not even when you found that heart flower about a month ago. They didn't come and that's weird. And Damara is too quiet. She must be plotting something big."

I walked out the water, and grabbed my towel from one of the rocks. "I know. I keep thinking about it too."

It really was weird. After Damara's last attack, I kept expecting her to show up at the enclave with her army and wipe us out. But the days passed, turning into weeks, which turned into months. Right now, I was just content we seemed to be at peace.

Letting out a long sigh, I wrapped my towel around my body. "I know she'll attack at some point. That's why we increased security around the enclave, and we've been training a lot." Thankfully, I had improved in hand combat, thanks to Kane and his immense patience. "We'll be ready."

Trina shook her head. "I think she'll attack tomorrow."

I stilled. "What?"

"Think about it. We'll all be distracted and celebrating. It's the perfect time for her army to strike."

"That's a valid concern," Kane said, walking out of the water. He had swimming trunks on, and nothing else. Although Trina probably knew every inch of his body, I didn't like him parading his hotness in front of her like that. Especially when I caught her stealing glances at him. Like now. Irritated, I threw the second towel to him. He caught it with one hand. "I'll make sure to bring that up with Theron, and we'll work on reinforcing security for tomorrow."

Since Artan fled the enclave with Kizzy two months ago, Theron had become the leader of the warriors. He hated answering to the council, but besides Artan, he was the best.

And though Kane hadn't joined the rank of warriors officially, he helped every opportunity he got.

"I have a bad feeling about tomorrow." Trina pressed her hand over her chest. "Just … be ready."

Kane patted his shoulders with the towel, hiding most of his torso behind it. "We will."

After glancing at me again, Trina marched out.

I stared at the spot she walked into the trees before disappearing into the forest for a few seconds. "Do you think she's right?"

Kane stalked to me. "I don't think so, but there's no reason why we can't bring that up to your brother and increase security. Better safe than sorry."

Damara wouldn't dare attack us on such a special day, would she? She was evil, she was mad, but she was still a tzigane, wasn't she? She also needed the heart flower to feed her madness and defy time. That was the only way she was over two hundred years old and still alive.

Kane was right. I shouldn't worry about it yet. Tomorrow was an important ceremony for me, for all of us, and I would focus on what I had to do—nothing else. I would leave the security problems and worries to the warriors.

I stared at Kane, totally mesmerized. The sun was starting its descent, tinting the sky with pinks and oranges. The water droplets on Kane's body gained a golden hue, and he looked as if he were made of gold.

By Saint Sara-la-Kali. Would my desire for him ever lessen? I seriously doubted it.

I cleared my throat. "Hungry?"

Kane put his heavy arm over my shoulders and pulled me into his side. "Always." I chuckled. That was true. Maybe it was his height and strength, but the man ate as much as a horse. "But how about if I cook tonight?"

I smiled at him. "How about you let me help?"

He placed a kiss on top of my head. "Deal."

After grabbing his swords from the rock—he never went anywhere without them—Kane slid his hand into mine and guided us back to my cabin at the edge of the enclave. Walking like this, with him, after a nice swim at the lake, I could almost pretend we were a normal human couple with no other worries in the world. Just us.

But as tziganes, our worries only increased.

Halfway down the forest path leading back to the enclave, we heard footsteps and the crunching of twigs to our side. On high alert, I channeled my fire, and Kane drew out his swords.

Darcy yelped as she stepped onto the path and saw us. "By Saint Sara-la-Kali." She hugged the wicker basket in her arms tight. "You almost gave me a heart attack."

"We thought you were an intruder." I extinguished my fire, and Kane lowered his swords. "Sorry."

The old hag narrowed her eyes at me. She was the head of the elder council and mother of the *rom baro*, the leader of the enclave—not to mention Artan's grandmother. I knew she had disliked me from the moment she first met me, and the feeling was mutual. I had always butted heads with her without any resentment, but lately, I had been honestly afraid of her. I was sure she knew I had the fire heart fever, and yet she either hadn't told the rest of the council, or she had and they were waiting for the madness to show up before taking me away and killing me.

The old hag brushed her long white braid back. "Have you trained today?"

I sighed. "Yes, I trained all morning."

Her gaze shifted to Kane, then the towels in our hands, then back to me. "Don't you think you should have trained all afternoon too, and gotten ready for the ceremony tomorrow?"

How could someone get on my nerves so much? "I'm ready, Darcy, don't worry."

She tsked. "If only we didn't need the heart flowers ..." Shaking her head, she stalked away, taking the path back to the enclave.

I gawked at Kane. "Was that a threat? That was a threat, right?"

He stared me, serious. "No, I don't think so."

He was lying.

I pointed in her direction. "I told you she knows about the fire heart fever. That *was* a threat."

Kane wrapped his arms around my back and pulled me to him. "Don't worry, Mi. While I'm with you, the fire heart fever won't get you, and I have no intention of ever letting you go."

2

"I haven't seen one of these in years," my mother said. She walked in front of Kane and me, leading us through the forest as if we didn't know the location of the festival's site. "Tziganes hold the spring festival every year, but this is the first time we'll actually perform the ceremony." She glanced over her shoulder at me.

I rolled my eyes. She was so damn proud that her daughter was the heart maiden and performing the ceremony at the festival for the first time in over two hundred years.

Yeah, no pressure.

Kane squeezed my hand. "She'll do great, Marisa," Kane said.

Although in the beginning my mother had been wary of him, since a heart maiden wasn't supposed to be touched, Kane had won her over easily. Now she didn't mind that we were together. Her only request was that we kept our relationship hidden. Otherwise, Kane and I risked the full wrath of the elder council—and I knew she meant what had happened to Damara and Emilian, her lover. Two hundred years ago, they had fallen in love, and when the council found out about it, their relationship was considered a crime. Emilian was executed, and Damara had killed herself. Or so everyone thought. In reality, she had run away. In her despair, she collected all the heart flowers she found, kept their powers for herself, surrendering to the madness the magic brought on, and learned how to extend her life.

I didn't think I would surrender to the madness and live off revenge for two hundred years if the elder council got Kane, but I was sure I wouldn't sit idle either.

I was also sure my mother was afraid of that—of what I would do to the council and anyone else who crossed my path.

I suppressed a shudder.

"Are you cold?" Kane asked, pulling me closer.

My heart tugged. He was always so perceptive of me. It made me feel so loved and safe.

"You know I have ways of sending the cold way." To illustrate my point, I sent my fire to our joined hands, warming my skin up. And to show me it didn't burn him, Kane tightened his grip around my hand. It still amazed me how he could feel the heat, but even when my fire was so strong to the point of burning someone else's skin off, it didn't hurt him at all.

He brought my scolding hand to his lips and pressed a kiss on the top of my orange skin. "I really like your neat tricks." Smiling, I let go of the magic and my fire retreated. Kane leaned over me and whispered in my ear, "You look beautiful." I cocked an eyebrow. "I mean, you're always beautiful, but today ..." His eyes ran the length of my body, desire glinting in his eyes. "You're stunning."

My cheeks warmed.

I had applied makeup and dressed up for the festival—a long dark red skirt paired with a black top with golden embroidery, red, gold, and black bracelets lined my arms, big golden hoops in my ears, and a thin golden bandana on the top of my head—but hearing his compliment made me feel good. Happy. Satisfied.

I smiled at him. I hadn't said anything, but he was looking mighty handsome in a more dapper version of his black leather clothes, with his twin swords securely strapped to his back. "And you're looking damn hot, as usual," I whispered.

Kane showed a lopsided smile that made my heart beat faster. "I always do."

I rolled my eyes and he let out a faint chuckle.

"We're almost here," my mother announced, catching our attention.

According to the elder council, the festival had to be set up on high ground, which was why it was a few miles north of the enclave, at the top of a hill halfway through a mountain. It was a vast area, enclosed by thick trees and flowering bushes, making it perfect for the spring festival.

I had seen and participated in all the planning and the schedule of the festival, and yet, I hadn't seen it all put together. That was why I gasped once we broke through the trees and arrived in the clearing.

Big, open-sided tents in red, orange, and burnt yellow or gold had been erected on the hill, each one held long wooden tables full of food and drink. In between the tents, lanterns had been strung, forming a colorful corridor. Every few feet, wooden posts were erected with sconces for the torches to be lit later in the day, once the sun began to set. On one side, a small wooden stage had been set up, and musicians got ready with their Spanish guitars and other instruments. Right in front of it, a large square of flat wood had been placed as the makeshift dance floor. Beside it, tziganes in flamenco dresses and shoes got ready to dance. On the other side, vendors formed long corridors, where tziganes could show off their talents by selling paintings, jewelry, small furniture, clothing, and whatever else they could do. And right in the middle of it all, atop the hill, was a big, unlit bonfire with a black cauldron hanging above it—that was where I would perform the ceremony later today.

Amid it all, tziganes walked and chatted and laughed, while kids ran around, playing and dancing and giggling.

A warmth that didn't come from my fire wrapped around my heart.

This was beautiful.

"I'm glad we increased security," Kane said, eyeing the place. "It's much bigger than I thought it would be."

"Oh, it is," my mother said. "Especially since there's a real heart maiden performing the ceremony." She looked at me, pride shining in her eyes. "Other enclaves are coming later today to see you."

The warmth was gone, quickly replaced by worry. More tziganes were coming to see me? By Saint Sara-la-Kali ... what if I messed up? What if—?

"Stop those thoughts," Kane said. "I know what's going through that mind of yours and let me tell you: Stop right now. You know you can do it. It doesn't matter if it's one person watching or a thousand."

I stared at him, again ensnared in his web. How did he know me so well? It was amazing.

My mother scooted to my side. "He's a keeper," she whispered, looking at him. Kane's lips tugged upward at her compliment. "Although, you two should drop those." She grabbed our joined hands and broke them apart. "You know the elder council can't find out about you two, so be careful. Act like a precious heart maiden, and the warrior intent on keeping her safe. No more than that." She stared at Kane, then at me, her eyes full of concern. "Understood?"

I wanted to smile at her, at the proud and full feeling that expanded in my chest. All my life, my mother and I had been at odds. A handful of times, we had even stopped talking to each other, but since we made up two months ago, she had been the best. She accepted me the way I was, she didn't lie to me anymore, and she didn't hover like an overprotective mother either. Bonus points that she liked Kane and didn't tell us to stop our relationship.

Kane straightened, as if he was in front of a general. "Yes, ma'am."

"Ma'am, my ass," my mother grumbled.

I gasped. "Mom!"

Kane chuckled.

"Let's go," my mother said, pushing forward.

In ten steps, we were in the thick of the festival, and I was surrounded by tziganes. They kept saying how beautiful I looked, how young I was, how excited they were to see the ceremony.

Well, me too. Excited and starting to get super nervous about it.

"Come on," Kane whispered, nudging me forward.

I followed his lead and walk through the tents. Since I

stayed in motion, the tziganes didn't swarm around me; they stood as I walked by, greeting me, but not suffocating me.

Much better.

Although we couldn't hold hands, after the second tent we walked through, I realized it felt like Kane and I were on a date. We strolled side by side, we paused in front of the tables of food and drink, we picked at the food, and we made comments about the decorations, the location, the people.

My nerves were soon back to normal, and once more, I realized I had never been this happy before. Which brought back to mind Trina's words. Would Damara really attack tonight? She couldn't. She wouldn't. And even if she tried, Kane and Theron and the other warriors would stop her. I had to believe that.

"What's with the frown?" Kane asked as he handed me a glass of water. As much as I would love to drink wine right now, I had to think of the ceremony later. "What are you worrying about now? The ceremony? Damara? Or us?"

Trying to lighten the mood, I took the glass from him and raised an eyebrow. "Should I worry about us?"

The glint in his eyes darkened. "I want to kiss you so bad right now."

My insides melted. "I want that too." Clearing my throat, I took a step back. "You should try to keep your distance today, otherwise I'm not sure how long I can control myself."

Kane let out a low chuckle. "I could say the same of myself." He nudged me with his elbow. "Let's keep moving."

We did and soon walked by the tent where Felix was. When the elder council mentioned bringing Felix out and putting him into a large cage under a tent, so the tziganes could see the rare heart animal, I had refused. However, Felix didn't mind. He projected the image in my head of him being surrounded by curious, awed tziganes, and he liked the attention. So different from being locked in his—very large—cage at the corner of the enclave.

I paused and stuck my hand inside the cage, scratching his big head. Gasps echoed around me, and I realized that the tziganes were shocked by seeing someone touch the white lion. I was so used to it, I didn't remember that heart animals were usually guarded and didn't let anyone touch them. After telling Felix to be nice and let the kids caress him too, I resumed my stroll with Kane.

We soon saw my friends. Theron escorted Ellie from tent to tent, much like Kane and I were doing, but he kept glancing at the forest, as if expecting something to happen. Cora and Rye marched through the crowd, and from their straight shoulders and serious faces, I knew they were on patrol, not on a date. Tomas tried to patrol the area too, but Ryane followed him around, distracting him with food and drink and music and dance. Jayme, Leander, and Lash stood guard on the festival's perimeter. Bryna, who had just had her and Jayme's baby, was seated near the dance floor with Sheila, waiting for the dances to start. Anne ran around with the kids, and the always vigilant Maire followed her around from a distance.

Trina was the only one who didn't come forward, choosing to stay with the other warriors on the perimeter of the festival's site. Her eyes met mine, but she quickly looked away.

Neil was with Oscar and Darcy and most of the elder council, overseeing the details of the festival. I had expected to find them glaring at everyone and complaining about everything, but instead, they chatted animatedly and even laughed here and there.

At first, I had thought no one would enjoy this festival. How could they when a third of our enclave had been killed two months ago? But in the end, it was exactly what everyone needed to keep going, to keep pushing forward, to keep living.

But that didn't mean we forgot the dead. One of the largest tents had been assigned to honor the dead, not just the ones who perished in the recent attack, but everyone whose family wanted them remembered.

Kane and I walked through the tent, taking in the half walls with the many pictures and messages and dedications. My heart twisted especially after seeing Sloan's and Nico's memorials.

But where was Ramon's? I searched for his and didn't find it.

I approached Vano, the elder council member responsible for this tent. "Excuse me. Where is Ramon's memorial?"

The bald man stared at me from head to toe with pure disgust in his eyes. "He couldn't be honored by the tziganes."

I shook my head. "What? Why?" My mother, Dolan, Sheila, Theron, and I had spent days preparing pictures and messages, talking about Ramon, laughing and crying, while putting together our last goodbye to him. "I thought Dolan would have given everything to you."

"Oh, he did," Vano said. "But in the end, the elder council decided he was forbidden to have rituals and honor as a tzigane."

I felt the fire rising in my veins. "Why would you do that?"

"He was a werewolf," he spat. "His blood was tainted. He wasn't a real tzigane anymore."

"What—?" I advanced on the man.

Kane hooked his arm around my waist and spun me

around before I could burn the man's face. "Shhh," he whispered in my ear. He held me close, my back tucked against his chest. "Don't hurt him now. You'll only regret it later."

I jerked against his grip. "I don't care. I want to hurt him."

"Mirella," Kane said, his voice soft. "Think about it. Ramon wouldn't want you to hurt someone because of him."

My rage faded and my muscles sagged. By Saint Sara-la-Kali. I almost went berserk and attacked a council member, because my rage had gotten the best of me.

It was normal for my temper to act up, but I wasn't always this crazy, was I?

"Let's get out of here," I whispered.

With a hand secured at my lower back, Kane guided me away from the tent and into the open walkways again. Once we were under the colorful lanterns, I looked up, soaking in their bright colors and beauty, and beyond them, the blue skies, as I inhaled deeply.

Kane halted in front of me. "We can do something to honor your brother later."

We had already gotten together and done burial ceremonies for Ramon. This was something extra that the elder council had suggested we do, to appease any tzigane who felt it was too soon for a festival—but it wasn't like we could move spring. And I stupidly thought Ramon would be included in the mix.

"It's fine," I forced the words through my lips. "Wherever he is, he knows he's loved."

Kane offered me a small smile. "I wish I could hug you right now."

"Me too," I whispered. I looked around. "Maybe we can sneak out until the ceremony later." I beckoned my chin to the edge of the tent to our left, where it met the forest. "Like two teenagers."

Kane's smile widened. "You have a dirty mind."

I gasped, feigning innocence. "What? Me? No way."

"Come on, Mirella." Kane gestured down the makeshift street. "As heart maiden, you should greet everyone before the ceremony."

"I know, I know." I stepped to his side, and together we resumed walking down the path formed by the tents and stands.

Pushing aside my anger and sadness over Ramon and his missing memorial was hard, but I knew Kane was right. As the heart maiden, the other tziganes looked up to me—they were doomed—and I had to pretend to be a mature, wise, and calm woman for the next few hours.

It would be impossible.

"Mirella!" a voice squealed. I turned in its direction and my breath caught. Kizzy ran toward me. She didn't slow down until she slammed into me and wrapped her arms around me like she had always been my best friend and we hadn't seen each other in a long while. The later was true, but the former? Not so much. "It's so good to see you!"

I pulled back, still shocked. "What are you doing here?"

She smiled at me, her light brown curls swaying as if she was thrumming with happiness. "Oh, we couldn't miss the festival." We? Which meant ... Artan was here. My stomach dropped. "I have such big news to share."

I stared at her, afraid of what she was trying to tell me. "Hm, what news?"

"You know, every year at least one wedding is performed at the festival to welcome new life and a new bond to spring."

Her smile widened. She seemed so happy, I felt sick. "This year, it's my turn."

"W-what?"

She bounced on the heels of her foot. "Artan and I are getting married tomorrow morning, and as heart maiden, I would love if you would officiate the ceremony."

3

My heart raced, thumping against my ribs hard. "Hm, Kizzy, I can't—"

"Yes, you can," she said. "I talked to Darcy and Oscar. They said that as long as they teach you what to say, and later the *rom baro* signs the papers, it should be okay."

But I wouldn't be okay. Didn't she get it? She knew Artan and I had a complicated relationship. Why was she doing this to me?

"Look ..." The words died on my lips when Artan appeared beside Kizzy, looking at me as if I too was simply an old friend.

I stilled and Kane took a step closer to me, as if he knew I needed him to lend me his strength.

"Hi, Mirella," Artan said. His amber hair was cut shorter and his matching amber eyes were soft, calm. Was he really calm about this? "I gather Kizzy gave you the good news. We're getting married tomorrow, and she insisted on having you officiate it."

I leaned forward. "And you're okay with that?"

Kizzy chuckled. Was this funny? "Oh, Mirella, you're the most important tzigane in the world. How could we have anyone else marry us?"

Curse words flew to my throat, and it was all I could do not to spew them in her face. "I don't want to be rude, but I'm not sure that is a good idea."

Like a snake striking, Artan moved forward and grabbed my hand in his. All I could do was stare. "Mirella, I'm sorry things didn't work out, and that we ended up hurting each other, but I'm ready to move on. And as an offering of peace and friendship, I think it would be a great idea if you married Kizzy and me."

I snatched my hand from his grasp. He had moved on? I had moved on too! And I was happy! I wasn't appalled because I still had feelings for Artan—I didn't. All my feelings for him were now bittersweet memories—but because they had the guts to ask such a thing of me. I would rather be left alone. Shit, if I could, I wouldn't even attend their wedding. And now they wanted me to officiate it? How could they do this to me?

"I—"

"Please, Mirella, do it," Kizzy said, cutting me off. She clasped her hands together. "Don't make me kneel down and beg, because I will."

What?

"Mirella," Artan said. "Please, do it."

At that moment, Ryane and Tomas stepped into our circle.

"Do what?" Ryane asked nonchalantly. Her arm was hooked on her fiancé's and a smile touched her lips; she was clueless to our conversation.

"I'm curious too," Tomas said.

"Mirella will officiate our wedding tomorrow morning," Kizzy declared, as if it was a done deal.

Ryane gasped. "Really?" She turned to me. "You can do that? Oh, then you have to do ours too, when the time comes." She glanced to Tomas. "Right?"

Tomas nodded as if he had never heard a better idea before. "Of course."

"Tomas, shouldn't you be with us, patrolling the perimeter?" Cora asked, joining our group. Rye was right beside her.

Ryane shot her a fake glare. "We're on a date."

"This isn't the time to go on dates," Cora said, all business. "We need more warriors to help us."

Artan frowned. "Why? Have there been any disturbances?"

"No," Rye said. "But we would like to be prepared, just in case."

"I'll join you all," Artan said.

"Wait, but I thought you were taking a break," Kizzy said. "At least until the wedding."

"The wedding?" Cora asked. "When is it?"

"Tomorrow." Kizzy clapped her hands. "And Mirella is going to officiate it for us."

By Saint Sara-la-Kali.

Cora turned her eyes to me. "I didn't know you could do that. It sounds great."

"It will be," Kizzy said.

Rye nudged Cora's arm. "We should go back to the others."

"I'm going with you," Artan said.

"Mirella and I should be going too," Kane said. He put a hand on my back. "She still hasn't greeted everyone who came out to see her, and the elder council asked her to do that before the ceremony tonight."

Without waiting for a reply from my friends, Kane pressed on my back and pushed me forward.

Once we were out of the circle, I inhaled deeply, as if I hadn't been able to breathe properly since Kizzy hugged me. But the rush of fresh air inside my lungs didn't do much to help with the sudden dizziness I felt.

I barely noticed as Kane slipped his hand in mine and pulled me to the back of a tent where paintings and other artwork were being displayed. He found a chair and pulled it behind a thick tapestry, trapping us in a small secluded corner. With his heavy hands, he pushed me down in the chair.

The next second, he was gone, and I found it was even harder to breathe if he wasn't near me. But then he came back, with a glass of water and a slice of sweet bread.

I drank the water in one go, but I held on to the bread, not hungry.

"Thanks," I said, finally meeting his eyes.

Kane knelt in front of me. "Feeling better?"

Was I? I didn't know why I was so upset, but I couldn't control the shock and the distress that took hold of me. I kept digging in, trying to find any resilient feelings for Artan, but all I felt was a great sadness over how bad things had gone for us. In some ways, I would always hold him dear, but that was it. I was sure I didn't love him anymore.

But that didn't mean I wanted to put up with his crazily excited fiancée and marry the two of them.

"I'm sorry," I whispered. "I didn't mean to get this upset. Please, don't misunderstand it."

"And how should I understand it?" he asked, his voice letting out a small edge of the hurt he was trying to hide.

"Imagine if it was Trina asking you to marry her and a super happy and almost annoying guy. Would that feel normal to you?" I asked, though I wasn't sure how he would feel about it. Trina and Kane hadn't really loved each other, but she had cheated on him and broke his heart nonetheless.

A long breath pushed past his lips. "No, it wouldn't. I would probably be shocked too."

"And I'll kill you if someday you decide to have me officiate your wedding too," I said with a small chuckle. I had gone for a joke, but Kane didn't laugh.

Instead, he leaned into me, his hands snaking up my arms, his eyes on mine. "You're the only one for me," he whispered before capturing my mouth with his.

By Saint Sara-la-Kali. I parted my lips and gave him all access he wanted. He kissed me hard and deep, and I was sure the kiss would leave a bruise on my lips, but I didn't care. As long as he stayed with me and gave me what I needed, I didn't care.

I was sure he was the only one for me too.

I scooted to the edge of the chair, getting closer to him. I wanted my body to touch his, every inch of it, even if there were clothes in the way.

I wanted to lose myself in his kiss. In him.

But in the distance, a couple of voices filtered through my muddled thoughts.

"The sun is going down. "

"So is it soon?"

"Yes, they are calling everyone to the bonfire."

"The ceremony should start soon."

"Oh, I can't wait."

Slowly, Kane broke the kiss, but he kept his firm grip on me, his forehead resting on mine. "It seems we have to go."

I nodded. "Unfortunately."

Kane's lip tugged up in an amused grin. He shot up and extended his hand to me. "Come on, heart maiden. Let's show your magic to everyone."

DARCY AND SHEILA HAD BEEN RUSHING THROUGH THE TENTS, looking for me. Sheila fretted if I was fine, but Darcy gave me an earful about disappearing like that. She went on and on about how I should grow up already, accept my responsibilities, and make the tziganes proud.

I didn't retort. What for? To argue about everything and get nowhere? Right now, I was tired of it.

Instead, I let her drag me to the hill, where every tzigane and bird and bee and ant gathered around the bonfire. My steps faltered when I realized there were too many people here. Seeing them walk around the festival had been one thing. Now that they were all gathered here, ready to watch me? It was intimidating.

I felt like a limb had been taken from me when Kane stayed behind—Darcy's orders—beside my mother and Dolan, and I had to walk through the crowd with Darcy. The moment the tziganes saw me, they cheered. Some even stood up and clapped. What was wrong with them? Was I receiving some award? Was I a famous actress? Their queen?

"Here you are," Darcy said, pointing at the unlit bonfire. The cauldron was much bigger up close and, for some reason, quite intimidating. She gestured to the small auxiliary table to the side. "And here are the supplies." She then turned her cold eyes to me. "You know what to do."

Why did that feel like another threat, as if she had said, "If you make a mistake, I'll kill you." I had rehearsed the ritual a few times before. However, because of the special ingredients it took, I had never done it for real. She had supervised most of those rehearsals; she knew I could do it.

The crowd quieted and sat on the ground or the benches or chairs spread around the hill top. At the edge of the festival camp, I could see the warriors patrolling the perimeter. They kept glancing this way, probably eager to see this part of the festival too.

Then, on the horizon, the sun dipped behind the trees.

Oscar came forward and lit the bonfire. "Let's begin!" he shouted as the fire roared to life.

The crowd cheered, sending a chill up my arms.

Oscar stepped back and joined Darcy on the ground a couple of feet behind me.

And just like that, the stage was mine.

I closed my eyes and focused. I called my magic and thought of spring bringing warmth to this icy cold land, but most of all, I thought of heart flowers blooming left and right, making my life as the heart maiden easier.

When I opened my eyes, I pushed my powers out to the bonfire. The fire billowed high, crackling and sparking. The crowd let out an amazed, "Oooh!"

As I had rehearsed, I turned to the side table and opened the wooden box on top of it, revealing a few pieces of the heart flowers I had found since I had become the heart maiden. I had no idea the center of the flower wasn't used in the heart elixirs—Trina and I had certainly used it in the potion she had made to save the tziganes two months ago—

and, anticipating this festival, Darcy had also saved a petal or two.

I grabbed the buds and petals in my hand, and as Darcy had instructed, I slowly spun around, showing the crowd I could touch the heart flower and its parts and it wouldn't melt away.

I halted in front of the cauldron again.

"Go, Mirella," I heard from my right. I glanced that way, and my heart wilted when I saw Kizzy kneeling on the ground beside Ryane and Lala, clapping hands as if she were ten years old and watching the best act at a circus. "You can do it."

I frowned and my thoughts went south. Images of her dressed in white coming down the aisle to meet Artan at the altar and poor me dressed like a priest, waiting for them. As if tzigane weddings went like that.

No, no. I shook my head slightly. I couldn't have thoughts like that right now. Darcy and Sheila had told me a thousand times that all my thoughts had to be about my magic, spring, and the heart flower. Nothing else.

Shit.

I closed my eyes again, and forced my mind to go back to the matter at hand. The festival, the ceremony, the cauldron.

I snapped my eyes open and threw the buds and petals in the cauldron, making a great show with my gestures, just like Darcy had demonstrated, insisting it was part of the spectacle.

Instantly, a small explosion came from the cauldron and colorful smoke rose from it, floating like a magical rainbow to the sky.

Just what I had been told would happen.

It had worked! I had done it!

A loud cheer started as pride filled my chest.

Until a crackling sound came from the cauldron. Everyone quieted down. A rapid sequence of *pop pop pop* began as the cauldron shook. As if it were alive, it sputtered a few tails of black smoke, before returning to the rainbow one.

"What was that?"

"Was that part of the ceremony?"

"Did the heart maiden do something wrong?"

"She messed up. I'm sure of it."

The crowd grew agitated and I grew worried.

By Saint Sara-la-Kali, I had messed up.

Darcy quickly came to stand beside. "It's okay, my friends," she bellowed. The chattering became a trail of murmurs. "There was a little hiccup with our spell, but as you can see, the smoke rising from the cauldron is the right color. The ceremony worked."

Despite her reassurance, everyone looked at me a little skeptical.

Oscar stepped up. "My friends, new beer kegs are being brought at this moment. Let's celebrate."

At the mention of free drink, the crowd cheered again and quickly dissipated, heading for the tents where they could find the drinks. Music filled the air as the band hopped on the stage and played flamenco songs, and the dancers took up the dance floor and started their show.

Darcy turned to me, her brows curled down. "I don't know what that was, but it wasn't right. You did something wrong. Where did you mess up?"

"I don't know," I lied. I knew that the problem was when I looked at Kizzy and thought of her and Artan. The sadness and frustration from before had returned and taken over my mind. A big mistake. "Is it bad?"

"We don't know," Oscar said, sounding disappointed. "There's no way of knowing right now." He waved me off. "Go around and show yourself to our people. They still love you and want to spend time with you."

And just like that, I had been dismissed.

Oscar and Darcy left with the rest of the elder council members, but I remained before the cauldron, staring at the rainbow smoke coming out of it.

My mother, Sheila, Dolan, and Kane approached me.

"It's okay," my mother said, putting her arm around me. "I bet that didn't mean anything."

"Yes." Sheila nodded. "That spell hasn't been done in so long, it was bound to have a few hiccups. But it's all right now. You did it."

"You should be proud of yourself," Dolan said. "We are." My father wasn't a man of many words, but I could see in his eyes that he meant it.

"We're going to find some place to sit down and have dinner together." My mother grabbed my hand in hers. "Come with us."

I slipped my hand free of hers. "I'll be right there."

From the corner of my eyes, I saw as my mother, Dolan, and Sheila exchanged worried glances.

"Okay," Sheila said. "We'll be waiting for you."

With slow steps, they retreated from the hill and disappeared into the closest tent.

Kane stepped to my side. "Want to talk about it?"

"No."

"What can I do for you, then?"

I looked up at him. He didn't seem fazed or worried about the shit I had done, but more than that, I was glad he didn't ask me what had happened. I was ashamed of myself. For messing it up and for the reason behind the mess up—because I was thinking of Artan and Kizzy. If I was going to mess it up, then it should have been because I had Kane on my mind and couldn't wait to get hot and heavy with him ...

A long breath deflated my chest. "Just take me out of here."

4

Sleeping in Kane's arms always made me feel better.

The next morning, I woke up reenergized. The ceremony had gone almost smoothly, the rainbow smoke had filled the skies until late into the night, and no one had attacked us.

So far, the festival was running great.

Until Ryane burst into my cabin, crying that Kizzy was having a tantrum and wanted me with her while she got ready.

"W-what?" I asked, standing before my closed bedroom door. I had joked that Kane should get dressed and escape through the window, and I was mildly concerned he had done it. I tightened the robe around my body. "She wants what?"

Ryane averted her eyes, her hands twisting into themselves. "We're all together at my *puri daj*'s house, getting ready."

"Who is we?"

"Kizzy, Kizzy's mother, my *puri daj*, Lala, Zara, and me."

I crossed my arms. "And she wants me there too? Why?"

Ryane shrugged. "She said you're a good friend and an important figure, and that you needed to be there for her during her special day."

My stomach twisted with knots. This was *not* happening. "I'm sorry, Ryane, but I have a to-do list a mile long. I have too many things to check before the ceremony in a couple of hours and—"

"Mi, don't you know how brides are on their wedding day?" I blinked. I really didn't know. Smiling, she went on, "They are excited and nervous and emotional and a ball of nerves. They can cry in happiness and scream of stress in the same sentence. That's why we always try conceding to all the bride's wishes before the wedding."

I pointed at my chest. "And her wish is to have me there right now."

"Yes!" Ryane nodded eagerly. "Come on. Ditch the to-do list. Do this for Kizzy and Artan. I know he's a good friend of yours. Don't you want him to be happy? For that, his bride has to be happy."

I pressed a hand to my stomach. How much longer would these people test my temper? They well knew how explosive it could be. Everyone suffered.

The problem was that only a handful of people knew what had happened between Artan and me. Almost no one knew how we had fallen for each other and broken each other's heart. To everyone else, Artan had always been a good friend and the trustworthy warrior in charge of the heart maiden's protection.

What I detested the most about this entire situation was that I was ready to forget all about it. I already had. Like a cut that healed long ago leaving behind a thin white scar, a mark that would never disappear. However, these people insisted on cutting the scar open and rubbing salt in the wound.

"I don't know," I said, exhaling. I didn't want to be a bitch and say no without a good reason, a reason I could explain.

Ryane entwined her fingers together and batted her lashes at me. "Please."

By Saint Sara-la-Kali.

I let out a long breath. "I will go, but on one condition."

Ryane's smile was almost too much for me. "What is it?"

"Ellie has to come with us."

<hr>

OF COURSE, ELLIE HATED THE IDEA.

"Are you really throwing me to the lions like that?" she whispered, as we walked from Theron's house, where she had been staying, to Darcy's.

"I didn't have much of a choice," I whispered back.

After I accepted Ryane's requested and stated my condition, I told her to go ahead while I gathered my stuff and got Ellie. With a skip in her step, Ryane left and I sneaked back into my bedroom. As I expected, Kane was up and fully dressed in his usual black leather armor-biker clothes, but thankfully, he hadn't jumped out the window.

"You don't need to go," he had said.

"I don't think I have much of a choice," I replied. Which was probably true. If Kizzy was having tantrums, then it meant that it was only a matter of time before Darcy came to call on me, and I certainly didn't want that.

The downcast expression of his handsome face made me realize I wasn't the only one hurting here. He probably didn't like Kizzy and Artan dragging me into their business, when all I wanted was to let them go. Kane was trying to hold on to me, but there were too many things pushing him away.

I was determined to stay close to him, though. Not only because he was the only one who seemed to be able to neutralize the symptoms of the fire heart fever, but because I wanted to be with him. For him. For me. I liked us together. I was happier when I was with him.

Once this festival was over, I would forget about Kizzy and Artan, wash my soul clean of them, and dedicate my heart and soul to Kane and me.

That made me feel better.

Thinking about that and Ellie, about how in the last two months she and I had dug up our friendship from the fiery pits of hell and become best friends again, made me feel immensely better.

Until Ellie and I arrived at Darcy's house.

The old hag opened the door for me. "Oh, thank Saint Sara-la-Kali, you're here." She snatched my arm and pulled me inside.

The women—Lala, Zara, Jaelle, and Ryane—flocked around Kizzy, who stood on a stool in the middle of the living room. She was dressed in a beautiful white gown with golden and red details. The top part had a peasant feel to it, with the top covering only half of her shoulders, and the skirt had several layers of fabric like a flamenco dress.

Her hair was pulled up but worked into a thick braid with red flowers weaved through it, and her makeup was subtle and elegant.

She looked beautiful.

"Mirella!" Kizzy shrieked when she saw me. She jumped from the stool and tripped on her skirt. The women screamed, and I reached for her, but she regain her footing easily. "You're here." She hugged me tight. "I'm so glad. Thank you for coming." Without letting go of me, she patted Ellie's shoulder. "You too. I'm so happy you're all here."

I glanced at Darcy and mouthed, "What happened?"

Darcy exhaled. "She was nervous," she said in a low voice. "We had to give her something."

"Tequila," Jaelle, Kizzy's mother, said. "We gave her tequila."

Kizzy pulled back and smiled at me. "I wanted more, but they won't give it to me."

"It's okay," I said, trying to smile at her too. "After the ceremony, you can have as much as you want." I put an arm around her shoulders and steered her back to the stool. "Let's just finish getting you ready first."

After two steps, Kizzy halted and stared at me. "Mirella, you're such a great person. You're gorgeous, you're kind, you have a good heart, you're strong, and you're special. I mean, it doesn't get more special than being the heart maiden, does it?" She placed a hand over her heart and her eyes filled with tears. "And you're a great friend. The best."

Holy shit.

I opened my mouth, not sure what to say to her, when thankfully Darcy got her from me and pushed her up the stool. "That's enough, Kizzy. Let's get you ready so we all can get ready next."

Watching as Darcy and the others fussed over drunk Kizzy, I retreated a few steps, still in shock with it all—being here, seeing Kizzy this drunk right before her wedding, and Kizzy's words. Was she being sincere? She was drunk, which meant the words flowed easier, but usually they were more honest. I certainly didn't feel gorgeous, kind, strong, or special.

I was just Mirella, a girl with a bad temper and a dirty mouth who got into messes because she acted with her heart before her head.

Ellie stood by my side and asked in a low voice, "How are you feeling?"

"I've been better," I confessed.

She grabbed my hand in hers and squeezed. "Just hang in there, my friend. This shit show is almost done."

BY THE TIME WE HEADED BACK TO THE FESTIVAL SITE, AND I stood once more at the top of the hill—but this time on a platform at the end of a long white carpet flanked by hundreds of chairs—I wished I had taken a few swallows of that tequila.

If not the entire bottle.

After Kizzy was ready, she practically passed out on Darcy's couch. Which had been a little worrisome because we had to retouch her makeup and hair after her power nap, but it had given us time to get ready too.

The chairs quickly filled up with tziganes—family and friend and the guests from other enclaves. I felt self-conscious beside Darcy and Oscar as we watched everyone settle in. It was as if they expected me to mess up the wedding after yesterday's gaff of the ceremony.

They probably thought I was a shitty heart maiden.

They weren't too far from the truth.

Like the night before, the warriors didn't join the ceremony. They patrolled the perimeter of the festival, stealing glances this way every few minutes. I was sure all of them wanted to be here with Artan, who had been their leader and friend for many years.

Instead of taking a seat with my mother and Dolan and Sheila and Ellie, Kane opted to join the warriors to make sure the festival remained a peaceful gathering. More than the other warriors, Kane glanced my way, probably worried about me.

Damn, I was worried about myself.

"It's time," Darcy said in a low voice, and just like that, she strolled down the long aisle, to the beginning.

Then Artan appeared beside her.

My heart skipped a beat. Looking every inch as regal and warrior-like in a stylized white tzigane garb, Artan took his grandmother's hand and slowly marched down the aisle. He didn't glance in my direction once, not even when he halted two steps from me. He simply turned his back to me and waited for his bride.

Why did this hurt?

Oh, I knew why. Because I shouldn't be the one doing this. I shouldn't be officiating my ex's wedding. That wasn't how life was supposed to go.

Complete silence fell around the hill.

Kizzy and her father appeared at the end of the aisle. Despite her tequila fiasco earlier, she did look beautiful and happy. And despite my reluctance and awkwardness in doing this, I was happy for the two of them. Or at least, I was trying to be. Because they deserved to be happy.

Just like someday, in some alternate reality, I deserved it too.

My eyes shifted to where Kane stood at the bottom of the hill. Maybe I could be happy with him. My heart squeezed in anticipation, and a smile took over my lips.

With Kane and our future together in mind, I was sure I could do this. I could marry my ex and his bride, and I could honestly wish them a happy life together.

Side by side, Artan and Kizzy stood in front of me, and for a moment there, I doubted my resolution. So I used a trick. I imagined them as two strangers. Using my magic, I blurred my sight, enough so when I looked at their faces, I could pretend they were John and Jane Doe.

I went through the ceremony as Darcy had taught me that morning: addressing all tziganes, telling them how it was such a splendid day for a wedding, talking to the couple about their responsibilities to each other, blessing them in Saint Sara-la-Kali's name and magic, handing them the Chalice of Eternal Love so they could share their first drink as a couple, and a new twist—saying a prayer of blessing and happiness as the heart maiden and enveloping them in my magic. The crowd seemed to love that, and Kizzy smiled wide at me.

Then, it was time for the *rom baro* to step in and finish it. He came forward with a heavy ledger and dropped it on the table. The pages were already filled with the promise of marriage and Oscar's signature. I signed as a witness, then Artan and Kizzy signed as the newlywed couple.

And just like that, in less than half an hour, Artan and Kizzy were officially married.

Oscar lifted his hands high and smiled at the tziganes. "My son is married! Let's celebrate!"

With loud chatter and laughter, the tziganes got up and headed to the tent where the reception had been set up. They could greet the newlyweds there and also drink and eat and dance—just like they had been doing since the spring festival had started.

My mother, Dolan, and Sheila waved at me before following the others. Ellie lagged behind and gave me a thumbs up, before my mother called her and she hurried away with them.

Wishing they would wait for me, I stepped off the platform, but Kizzy grabbed my arm, preventing me from going any farther. "*Nais tuke*, Mirella." She pulled me into a tight hug. "You're really a great friend."

By her side, Artan cleared his throat. "Yes, *nais tuke*." A small smile appeared on his lips. "That trick with your magic, that was cool."

"Yes! I loved that." Kizzy beamed. She hooked her arm on mine. "Let's go dance."

I pulled my arm from her grip. "I'll be there soon," I said, suddenly needing some distance from the two of them. I was proud of how I had handled myself so far, but I could only take small doses of this crazy situation. I needed a break before joining the reception. "I need to check something first."

"Of course." Artan nodded. "We'll see you there." He steered a pouting Kizzy away.

I watched as they walked down the aisle again, this time as a married couple.

Artan was married.

Even if I still had feelings for him, it was truly over now.

"What is going through that beautiful head?" A smile broke across my lips as I turned in the direction of Kane's voice. With deliberate steps, he walked up the hill from the side. "From what I could see, you did a great job."

"Thanks," I muttered.

He took a step toward me, his eyes locked on mine. "I

didn't get a chance to tell you this yet, but you look so fucking hot."

Heat crawled up my cheeks. This morning, I had chosen a dark green dress that matched my eyes. It had a tight bodice and modest neckline—I wanted to look serious while offici-ating the wedding--but when I walked, a slit showed, revealing my bare leg. I confess I had Kane in mind when I chose my outfit.

I advanced toward him, but didn't touch him as I wanted to, in case someone was close by and watching us. "Do you want to be late to the party?"

One of his eyebrows arched up. "Hm, I li—"

"Mirella!" Eyes wide, Theron raced up the hill and skidded to a stop right next to me.

Unease curled in my stomach. "What is it?"

"I think it's trouble," he said, a concerned hint to his voice. "You should come see this."

5

SEEING THERON'S URGENCY AS HE GUIDED KANE AND ME DOWN the hill, the knots in my stomach only tightened. I asked what was going on, but he said it was better if I saw it with my own eyes. Whatever that meant.

Many things crossed my mind. The revenants and red alchemists were coming. Damara was at the edge of the forest, taunting me with a heart flower in her hand. Dragons and wyverns were ready to attack us. A group of humans hiking a trail got lost and stumbled onto our festival.

But I wasn't expecting what he showed me.

Halting beside the other warriors at the bottom of the hill, just past the festival tents, Theron pointed to the trees a few feet ahead of us. "That."

A gasp escaped my lips.

A patch of blackened dead earth slowly spread over to the bushes and trees, consuming and withering all plants in sight. A squirrel jumped from one blackening tree to another, but was caught by the darkness. It spread over his fur and took over his little body. The squirrel fell to the ground, dead.

We all took a large step back.

Horrified, I stared at the darkness eating up the earth. "W-what is that?"

"I don't know," Theron said.

"Whatever it is, it can't be good," Cora said.

I glanced to Trina. "Have you ever seen anything like this?"

She shook her head. "No, nothing like this."

"I have no idea what it is," Rye said. "But if we don't find a way of stopping it soon, it'll spread over the festival grounds."

"And when will it stop?" I asked, trying to make sense of this.

"We don't even know *if* it'll stop," Theron said.

"We should ask an elder," Kane suggested. "Someone must have at least heard of this before."

"I'll go get my *puri daj.*" Theron spun around, toward the tent where the party was being hosted, but he halted after one step. "I don't think we need to call them."

We all glanced up the hill.

The elder council and a handful of others marched down the hill, coming toward us—among them were Darcy, Oscar, Neil, Sheila, Dolan, and my mother.

"They must have noticed we were all gathered here and suspected something was wrong," Cora said.

I just hoped nobody else had noticed and the party hadn't been interrupted, not yet.

The group of elders halted beside us, and like us, they were shocked and confused upon seeing the earth dying like that.

"What is this?" my mother asked, glancing at me. "Do you know?"

I shook my head. "I wish."

"I know what it is," Darcy said, drawing all attention to her.

"What is it?" Dolan asked.

Darcy shifted her eyes to me. "It's Mirella's fault."

My breath caught. "W-what? What did I do?" Body stiff, Kane stepped closer to me, ready to squeeze the old hag's throat.

"That black smoke during the ceremony," Darcy said. "Something went wrong there, and now it's poisoning the earth, killing everything."

"How do you know?" Kane asked. "There hasn't been a heart maiden in two hundred years. You haven't seen this happening before."

"No, I haven't," Darcy said. "But I have read all the books and journals in the enclave's library. I know of things that happened two hundred, five hundred, a thousand years ago." She pointed to the earth. "And I know this was caused by the problem in the ceremony."

"She's right." Sheila sighed. I stared at my grandmother, feeling a little betrayed that she sided with the old hag. "I've also read about this before."

The blackened earth advanced another foot and we all took a large step back.

"Is there a way to reverse this?" Theron asked.

"Yes, I remember reading something about it before," Darcy said.

"What is it?" I asked, eager to undo my mistake.

"I'm not sure," the old hag said. "I don't remember. I'll need to check the books. Meanwhile ... Oscar, Neil, Sheila, Risa and Dolan, please calmly disband the party and send everyone to the enclave. We all should be safe there. For now." The five of them followed her order and rushed up the hill toward the tent. "Leander and Lash, stay here and monitor its advancement." Then she glanced at me again. "And Mirella, you're under house arrest."

I gasped. "What?"

Fist clenched, Kane stepped in front of me. "Why? Even if it was her doing, it was a mistake. She can help you fix it."

Darcy's hard gaze could cut through a rock. "Vano and Boldo," she called to two council members. "Take the master slayer away."

This time, I couldn't stay still. "What? Darcy, are you crazy?"

"I've put up with it for far too long," Darcy said, her rage clear in the sharpness of her words. "The heart maiden isn't supposed to be touched, and yet, you two have been together for the past two months."

My stomach dropped. "How ...?" And I thought we had been so careful.

"Touching the heart maiden is treason. Moreover, you're the reason Mirella didn't perform the ceremony correctly."

I blinked. "Excuse me?"

"You had this man on your mind, when you know you should have thought only of spring and the heart flower." She pointed to Kane. "Vano, Boldo, now." Kane stepped back, raising his hand in warning. Vano and Boldo stopped, but didn't retreat either. "Get him!"

Vano and Boldo drew their swords. Everyone stepped back, afraid of being struck by mistake, but I remained at Kane's side.

"Stop this," I said.

Boldo shook his head. "Sorry. We have our orders."

They advanced on Kane. I knew they would get their

asses kicked, so I stepped aside, not wanting to take part in that.

But as the fight began, Darcy sighed. "By Saint Sara-la-Kali." She pointed her hand at Kane. Her power made the air around us vibrate and press against Kane. He gasped for air as his chest was squeezed.

Panic grabbed hold of me. "Stop! What are you doing?" Kane fell to his knees and I knelt beside him. "Let him go!"

Trina stepped forward and glared at Darcy. "That's insane. He has been nothing but helpful. Stop it!"

Darcy didn't stop there. "And since we're cleaning house … Carlo and Gunari, take Trina away too."

Trina froze in place, in shock.

"What for?"

"Using alchemy when it's forbidden," Darcy said. "And don't think I don't know you've been doing more alchemy behind our backs." Okay, that was a surprise to me too, but that didn't give Darcy the right to make her, and Kane, prisoners. To torture them like she was doing. "Surrender before I have to hurt you too." The warriors Carlo and Gunari advanced on Trina. She retreated and used some self-defense moves to deflect their hands as they came for her. "You asked for it." In less than five seconds, Trina was on the ground beside Kane.

"Stop it!" I cried, channeling my power. I didn't want to attack Darcy, but I would. Oh, I would.

"Interfere and you're next," she warned.

The warriors grabbed Kane and Trina and started dragging them away. I felt like my heart was being ripped from my chest.

I opened my hands, calling for my fire.

Cora stepped in front of me. "Mi, no."

Theron held my arm back, gently. "Don't attack now. You'll only make everything worse." The pleading glint in his eyes got to me, and I let my fire fade.

A desperate sob rose to my throat. I glared at Darcy. "You're not just an old hag. You're evil."

She didn't seem fazed with my insult. "If I have to be branded as evil to keep this enclave running smoothly, so be it." She glanced to the remaining council members and marched away.

In the distance, the party had been disbanded and the guests calmly walked toward the enclave, completely unaware of the mess happening at the bottom of the hill.

To the side, Carlo, Gunari, and most of the warriors carried a disabled Kane and Trina away, and Darcy followed them with her trusty council members, holding herself like a queen.

And a few feet from me, the earth was dying and spreading across the land because of me. Would it stop? How far would it go? How fast? Would it kill everything and everyone? I had to assume it would keep spreading indefinitely until my mistake was fixed. It would kill the land and no heart flower would bloom again. Not around here at least.

A pang cut through my chest, and I thought I would faint from its pain. I pressed a hand to my heart. "What do I do?"

"First, we get out of here," Theron said. He looked at Leander and Lash. "Are you two okay?"

Leander nodded. "That was scary."

"Yes." Lash glanced at me. "Are you okay?"

I wouldn't lie. "Not really."

Leander put a hand on my shoulder. "Just so you know, we're on *your* side." I was glad to know he and Lash wouldn't betray me and my friends like the other warriors had done, but that still didn't stop the pain from taking hold of my chest. "Go and do whatever you have to do. We'll be fine here."

Theron patted his back. "*Nais tuke.*" He looked at me. "Let's go. Let's find out where they are taking Kane and Trina and come up with a plan to prove their innocence." He stole another glance at the advancing darkness. "And how to fix this."

It was too much. The wedding, Kane, Trina, the darkness. It was just too much. The pain pressed against my chest and spread to my head. "No," I whispered, cupping my head. This was not the time to have an episode. But I couldn't help it. The pain kept spreading, robbing me of my strength, and I folded to the ground.

6

"Mirella!" someone shouted.

I heard several voices at once, but none of them made sense anymore.

Unwelcomed images filled my mind.

Artan at the altar, waiting for me. But when I finally got there, he turned his back on me and kissed Kizzy.

Kane telling me it had all been a mistake and leaving me.

Trina hiding in a corner and doing alchemy.

Damara and her revenants and red alchemists attacking the festival and killing all the tziganes in sight.

Darcy condemning me to death for everything.

The darkness spreading and killing everyone who was still alive, including Felix.

Laughter filled my head, bringing more pain, and I was sure that laughter wasn't part of the hallucinations. That was Damara, laughing at me.

"Mirella," a voice filtered through the mess in my mind, but I couldn't discern it.

I couldn't even answer it.

The pain came back, stronger and deeper than it had ever been before, like a huge explosion inside my skull.

I blacked out.

I woke up with a jerk and everything came back to me in a flash. The wedding, the darkness, the accusations, the episode. I had had an episode and I was sure Darcy and the other council members had seen me, because I was now seated on a hospital bed in a square room with cold, white walls, no windows, and one thick metal door.

Panic spread through my veins and I shot up. My head swam, and I had to lean against the bed before I fell on the hard floor.

By Saint Sara-la-Kali.

Where was I? What was going on?

I glanced down at me. I was still wearing the same outfit I had chosen for the wedding, but I didn't have any of my rings and bracelets and earrings. And I didn't have any shoes. I grabbed my hair and sniffed. I could still catch a strong whiff of vanilla and coconut, which told me I hadn't been here for long. Unless someone had washed my hair while I was out.

I shook my head. Okay, time to focus. I had to find out what was going on.

On wobbly feet, I stalked to the metal door. I lifted my hand to bang on the door until someone came, but I never made it. The door opened before I touched it and Darcy stepped inside.

I narrowed my eyes at her. "You. What have you done?"

"What I had to," she said, closing the door behind her. She faced me, completely unafraid that I might attack her.

She should be, because I wanted to. She gestured to the space around us. "This underground room has held many heart maidens who have lost their minds. The walls and doors are reinforced with magic, so don't bother trying to break out."

I knew she knew about the fever. "When did you figure out I had the fire heart fever?"

"When we were at Kane's mountain house," she said. "I've been watching you even closer since then, and I'm amazed you haven't had any episodes ... until this morning." One corner of her lips curled up. "Since it was in front of your friends and several elder council members, I was able to act." She gestured to the room again. "And here you are."

"What about my friends? Where are my mother and my father?"

"They are all fine. They have been escorted back to the enclave, where they should be safe from the darkness for now. They think you had a breakdown due to stress and are now being treated."

"They will want to see me."

"Yes, they're already asking for you. To be honest, Theron didn't want to let go of you, but I was able to persuade them you need rest and quiet for now."

"What about Kane and Trina?" I asked, sure she wouldn't answer me.

"They have been detained too," she said simply.

Rage coursed through me. "You're evil."

"I'm not evil. I just have the guts to do what's necessary. For example, it is necessary to kill the heart maiden when she starts losing her mind." I held my breath. "I will kill you, but before that, we need to find a way of reversing your mistake and restoring the dead land."

"I'm assuming you didn't find anything in your books yet."

"No, but while I look for that, I have other methods." She knocked on the door. A moment later, it opened and Vano stepped in with a metal chair in his hand. "You can begin."

He let go of the chair and advanced on me.

"What?" I retreated. "What are you doing?" My back hit the wall, and I called my fire.

But it didn't answer.

"Don't bother," Darcy said. "When you were out, I gave you a potion to numb your powers. You won't feel them for a while."

My stomach hit the floor.

No, no, no.

Vano grabbed my arms, and as if I weighed no more than a rag doll, he pushed me down in the chair. I jerked and fought against him. I didn't have my magic, but I knew how to fight. But then, he landed a punch against my cheek. My head snapped to the side and pain spread over my face. Tears filled my eyes. I could barely breathe, and he took advantage of it to tie a rope around me—tight.

"What's this for?" I forced the words out my lips. The pain increased tenfold, and I instantly regretted saying anything.

"Vano's special power is to enter other people's mind," Darcy said. "He can find hidden memories."

"And what are you trying to find inside my mind?"

"Since we still don't know a way to fix the problem, we have to see what caused it in the first place," Darcy said.

My chest seized. That meant ... Vano would dig through my mind until he saw what Artan had meant to me. And he would tell Darcy about her precious grandson and how he had touched me too. "I thought you said it was Kane."

"It could be, but I was just making use of the opportunity presented to me."

She meant catching Kane and Trina. "You sicken me."

"I'm not worried about your opinion of me." She went on, "Anyway, after that, we'll search for a solution. Since you caused the problem, maybe your subconscious already knows how to fix it." She shrugged. "Or maybe we can find that out from Damara, through the connection you two share."

"And I'm sure this will hurt."

She tsked. "It could be done more gently, but since I know you're going to fight it, I told Vano to just push through it." She nodded at him. "Do it."

A second later, I felt the pressure of his hand pushing against my mind. I reinforced my walls. It was already hurting, but I wouldn't give in that easily. They wanted my memories? They would have to pry them from me.

Darcy had warned me this was Vano's special power, so I really didn't hope to win this battle, but I sure wanted to give him a run for his money.

He pushed harder through my walls. A boom echoed through my mind as the wall broke, and he came into my head like a bulldozer. I tried fighting more, or making it difficult for him to find anything, but it felt like he had five hundred hands digging through my skull and I was being buried in pain and confusion and misery. The more I resisted, the more it hurt.

"Keep fighting," Darcy said. "Suffer more because of your stubbornness."

What was my other choice? Just sit here and let them strip me bare and abuse my mind freely? That wasn't me. That was never going to me.

I pushed against Vano, giving him some trouble. But it

didn't take long for him to surprise me and take me down again.

He rummaged through my mind, going through memories not even I wanted to remember. My moments with Kane, Artan, and Phillip. Arguments with Theron and Ellie and my mother. My encounters with Damara and how I found out about the fire heart fever. My connection to Felix. The moment I found out Cianna was my *puri daj* and then how she died in my arms. When Ramon told me I was his half-sister, and later, how he died in the fire I had created.

Vano went further. He saw when I left my mother and moved to Broken Hill, how I was determined to make it alone, how I loved dancing, how I knew something was off about me, and how the alchemists kept showing up in my life. How Layla had died because of me and the same would have happened to Ellie, if I hadn't intervened.

He went back more, to the embarrassment I felt about my mother and how I tried to hide I was her daughter from everyone at school, because they teased me about her being crazy—I thought they were right. The times we moved around the country for seemingly no reason—now I knew it was because the alchemists were after us. To my secluded childhood and how my mother indoctrinated me to believe I couldn't trust anyone since I was a little kid.

He went on and on for hours, bringing physical and emotional pain with each assault.

I was practically passed out in the chair when, finally, Darcy called it off. Vano untied me. With no strength, I slipped out of the chair, but he caught me before I could hit the floor. He deposited on the cold bed and retreated.

"Rest. I'll send some food soon." Darcy exhaled through her nose, clearly annoyed. "We'll come back tomorrow."

Hadn't Vano seen my entire life already? Why did he have to do this tomorrow too?

Darcy and Vano left, taking the chair and rope with them, and shut the door with a definitive click.

Trying to regain control over my body, I curled into a ball. Tears brimmed in my eyes. I wasn't sure how much more of this I could take. Another session tomorrow? I think I would rather die.

I glanced around the room, searching for anything that could help me. A crack, an opening, something sharp that could be used as a blade, anything ... but there were just cold walls, the floor, and the bed, which was nailed to the ground, and sheets that seemed to be sewed to the mattress. If I tried to rip the sewing, I would only rip the fabric.

A long, defeated sigh escaped my lungs.

Darcy had said many heart maidens had been held in this room. Which meant ... Damara had probably been held here too, and somehow, she escaped.

Damara had always told me she had one big advantaged over me: She embraced the madness and the hallucinations. She let them consume her. Maybe that way, she was able to see a way to escape that I couldn't.

Did I have another choice? I couldn't see anything else.

Mourning myself, I took in a deep breath and followed Damara's advice. I stopped resisting and let the madness take over me.

It wasn't as easy as I thought it would be.

The hallucinations didn't come immediately, and when I tried lowering my shield and contacting Damara, she didn't answer.

There was someone else I could contact though. I closed my eyes and sent my magic out to search for Theron's mind. But my magic bounced off the walls like a ball. This room must have a barrier against that too, so prisoners wouldn't be able to communicate with anyone outside.

A shudder coursed through my body.

Prisoners. Besides the heart maidens, how many people had been wrongly accused by the elder council? How many had been killed? I couldn't begin to understand how evil they were or why. Why were they doing this?

I barely slept through the night because of the pain and the panic I felt, which only increased when Vano and Darcy came back the next morning.

The torture session began anew, and I thought I would die at any moment.

While Vano dug through my skull, content in exploring my rebel teenage years, I felt a hallucination taking over me.

I instantly tensed to fight it, but then I relaxed and let it come. For a moment, I was confused by Vano's powers and what was coming from the fire heart fever, but soon I found out: My hallucination featured Damara, seated on a red velvet couch in what looked like the living room of a mansion. She smiled at me as if I were a camera.

"Having fun?" she asked, amused. "Answer me, Mirella."

I cleared my throat. "W-what?"

She rolled her eyes. "This isn't a hallucination, dear. This is a vision through our connection. Are you having fun while that tzigane nitpicks through your brain?"

I groaned. "I don't think I need to answer that."

"That's no fun." She pouted. "I don't want them to kill you." Should I be thankful? "That would be too easy and no fun for me. When it's the right time, I'll be the one to kill you." The way she said it like it was a promise ... another shudder ran through my body. "Here. I think I can give you a get-out-of-jail-free card."

"Wha—?"

Before I could utter my question, the world spun and I felt it. My mind stretched, reaching past the protection around the tiny room. My mind traveled to a place I knew, and I felt a familiar mind connect to mine.

Theron.

He froze. *Mirella?*

Yes, it's me.

Holy shit. How are you? Where are you?

I don't know. What do you know?

We were told you had a breakdown and were taken to a sepa-

rate side of the infirmary, where you're getting special treatment. Is that true?

I scoffed. *Depends on how you see it.* I didn't want to tell him about the mental torture sessions yet. *What about my mother? Our father? Ellie?*

They are here with me. Everyone is here. Sheila, Cora, Rye, Artan and Kizzy too. We just gathered at the house, trying to decide how we were going to find out more about you. Artan wanted to beg his puri daj *for information.*

She won't tell you anything.

Then ... what do we do?

I felt it. The connection failing, breaking apart.

I don't have much time. All I know is that I'm underground, probably under the infirmary or some other administrative building. It seems like a mix of mental hospital and prison, but I honestly haven't seen much.

We'll find you, he said in my mind, his words firm. True.

By Saint Sara-la-kali, I really hoped they would.

Don't trust anyone else. Especially the elder counc—

The connection was gone.

I was ripped from the mental link as if Vano had torn it apart. I screamed as the pain burned through me, bringing me consciousness.

Darcy stared at me as if she had seen a ghost. "How—?"

"I can't get back in," Vano said.

I hated to admit it, but Damara was the one reinforcing the walls around my mind. Right now, I was thankful because I wouldn't be able to withstand one second against him.

Later, I would push her away too. But not yet.

"That's absurd!" Darcy pointed to me. "Try again."

Vano pushed with all his might, but damn, Damara was strong. "I can't," he said, giving up. "She's resisting me."

Darcy glared at me. "Fine. Have your victory today. It won't last."

Stomping her feet, Darcy marched out of the room. Vano followed her and slammed the door. Even that clicking, locking noise sent a ringing pain through my head and I had to close my eyes.

You're welcome, Damara said in my head before retreating.

I didn't know what her game was, or why she was helping me—just so she could kill me later? That seemed petty, but I was too weak and desperate to complain or care.

As soon as she left me, I reinforced the walls around my mind with the strength I had left. My exhaustion won and I fell into a deep sleep.

———

I HAD NO IDEA HOW LONG I WAS OUT, BUT WHEN I WOKE UP, I called my magic to push the grogginess away and clear my mind—as much as it would since surrendering to the madness.

And I came up with a plan.

I stayed in bed, like a helpless girl, and waited.

A couple of hours later, my door opened and Carlo stepped into the room, carrying a tray with my dinner. I didn't have to pretend to be weak as I sat up on the bed and reached over to get the metal tray. I was actually hungry, and the scent of the chicken soup teased my nose, but I didn't surrender to it.

Instead, I acted.

I threw the contents of the tray on the floor and swung the tray at Carlo's head. He wobbled with the impact, and I took advantage of his dizziness to shoot up from the bed and hit him again.

He went down.

My stomach twisted with a sick feeling, but I didn't have time to regret anything as Gunari rushed into the room.

He looked from Carlo to me. "What the—?"

I swung the tray toward him, but he leaned back, missing being hit by an inch. He went for the sword at his waist. And I sent a spark of fire to his hands. He pulled them back with the burn. He tried again and I sent a bigger fireball. "You little bitch." He lunged at me, his hands reaching for my throat.

I lost it. The madness crawled up from the depths of my mind and took over. I didn't see anything else other than the red of my rage and fire. I was barely aware as I fought my way out of my room and into the long, cold corridor. At the end, it opened into a larger room, and the metal doors gave away to cells with bars.

Someone dangled by the wrists from chains screwed to the ceiling in the cell across the room.

My heart squeezed. "Kane."

8

A SOB BROKE THROUGH MY THROAT, AND MY VISION CLEARED AS the madness loosened its grip on me. I rushed to his cell and shook the bars.

"Kane!" I called, but he didn't move. His head was drooped forward, and his toes barely touched the ground. Another set of chains wrapped around his ankles.

By Saint Sara-la-Kali, what had they done to him?

Invoking my power, I grasped the bars and melted portions of it. Then, I kicked on the weak parts and the rest of the bars fell to the ground with a *clank*.

"Kane," I whispered, cupping his face. His head was heavy on my hands. Another sob choked me. I placed a hand over his chest and waited. His heartbeat was slow and faint. I didn't have much time.

I stood on tiptoes and tried reaching for the chains around his wrists, but he was too tall for me. I looked around, trying to find anything I could use to help me.

Since I couldn't reach, and it didn't look like there was anything I could step on, I used another method. I opened my hand, palm up and conjured a snake of fire. It flowed from my palm and floated through the air until it wrapped around the metal clasps encasing Kane's wrist. Hoping he was still immune to my fire when I played with it like this, I closed my hand, increasing its heat. The clasps melted away.

And Kane crumbled. I stepped into him, my arms around his chest, but he was too heavy for me and the only thing I did was soften his fall.

"Kane," I called him again. "Please, you have to wake up. I can't carry you like this."

"Then free me next." I jumped, turning toward the voice, ready to strike. In the next cell, Trina sat on the ground, her arms chained to the wall. She looked a little better than Kane. "I can help you carry him out of here," she croaked.

"I didn't see you there." I slowly laid Kane down on the rough stone floor, and stood, facing the bars between their cells. "Why didn't you say something before?"

"I just woke up."

Using the same trick as before, I melted portions of the bars, then kicked the rest until they fell, the sound echoing through the room. I cringed. Soon, several warriors and council members would be upon us, I was sure.

I knelt in front of Trina and laid my hand around the chains. "This might hurt."

She gritted her teeth, getting ready. "Just do it."

Slowly, I increased the power of my fire. Trina swallowed a scream as the metal around her wrists turned orange and her skin gained a red tint. I retreated my hands. "I can't do it. Not like this." Instead, I clasped the chains a few inches from the clasps and used my power there. I knew the heat would transfer through the metal, but at least she wouldn't feel the brunt of my magic directly on her skin. We would figure out how to take the clasps off later. The chains fell. "This will do for now."

"*Nais tuke*," Trina said, pushing up. She swayed to the side, and for the first time, I took a good look at her. There were purple bruises all over her face and arms. "Don't look at me like that. They were much worse to Kane."

My stomach swirled, and I was sure I would puke, even though I hadn't eaten properly since ... I didn't even know when.

I gave her a side glance. None of us were in good shape. "Are you sure you can help me?"

"Oh, if it means we're getting out of here, I'll find some damn strength; don't worry."

We crawled through the bars and went back to Kane's cell.

I knelt beside him and shook him. "Kane, wake up."

"He has been like that for a while," Trina said, her voice tight.

"What did they do to him? To you both?"

Trina shook her head. "I—" She gasped and pointed to the center of the room. "Mirella, look out!"

I shot up as two warriors charged into the room, their swords raised. I didn't think; I just raised my hands and shot fireballs at them, powerful enough to hit and hurt and keep them down, but not enough to kill. I would rather escape without killing anyone.

"We have to go." I crouched beside Kane. "Help me here."

It was hard and my muscles screamed at me, but Trina and I lifted Kane's limp body up and carried it between us. Thank Saint Sara-la-Kali, Trina was strong. As for me, I called on my fire and asked it to lend me strength. I was sure that without it, I would never be able to carry half of Kane's weight by myself.

Together, Trina and I started our grand escape—at a snail's pace because of Kane. But it didn't matter. I would rather the grand escape took five days, then leave here in five minutes without him.

Once we exited the cell rooms and entered the long corridor with metal doors, Trina and I halted.

"What happened here?"

My stomach turned, and I thought I would barf right there.

At least a dozen bodies of warriors littered the floor— mangled, torn in half, burned to a crisp. The scent of smoke and fire and burned meat filled my nostrils.

Terror clutched my chest. "It was me," I whispered, realizing I had entered a state of madness when I left my room and I hadn't really known what I had done until I saw Kane in his cell. I must have killed the warriors when they tried to stop me. "By Saint Sara-la-Kali."

"All right. Just ..." Trina wrinkled her nose. "Try to ignore the scent and look straight ahead."

"But—"

"You can think about it all you want later!" Trina glared at me. "Just ... swallow it and let's go."

She was right. Damn it, it hurt and it sickened me, but she was right. I couldn't stay here any longer. They would kill Kane, Trina, and me, if we stayed. Not to mention I was bound to slip into madness again and kill them all.

No, I had to get away from here.

We walked past the bodies, trying to not step on anyone. At one point, I was sure I stepped on someone's hand, and it disintegrated into ashes. Bile pooled at the back of my throat.

Finally, we crossed the corridor and got to the thick door at the end. I tried twisting the knob.

"It's locked."

Trina leaned Kane against the wall beside the door. "Stay here," she said, as she let go of him. I had to use my entire body to hold him up against the wall.

"What are you doing?" I watched her over my shoulder.

Trina had knelt beside the body of a warrior. "Looking for this." She pulled out a set of keys. With a small smile, she found a small key and opened the metal clasps around her wrists. She sighed in relief. "And this ..." She held up a larger key.

"Should open this door," I finished her sentence.

She rushed to the door and tested the key. A frown fell between her brows. "No, that's not it."

She returned to the bodies and searched for more keys.

Shit, we didn't have time for this.

I called my fire and let it fill my veins. I felt it rolling up and down my body, like lava coming down the mountain and destroying everything in its path.

Screaming, I threw my hand out and fire flew out like a missile, blasting the door away from its hinges.

"Damn, girl," Trina said.

"Just ... let's go."

She grabbed the sword of a fallen warrior, hastily strapped it to her waist, then rushed to me and resumed her position on Kane's other side. I could feel the adrenaline fading and the exhaustion taking over as we made our way around the corner. I would crash soon.

But not yet. I couldn't crash yet.

Trina and I crossed the door into a short hallway with a set of stairs at the end. There was our way out.

But, as we dragged our feet toward the stairs, the sound of heavy footsteps echoed through the walls. A second later, warriors climbed down the stairs, their swords in hand.

Without a word, Trina and I laid Kane's heavy body on the floor behind us. We only had time to turn before the warriors were on top of us. Trina pulled out the sword and I channeled my power.

I raised a half wall of fire between us. Trina looked at me like I was crazy. Yeah, I know, I was trapping us at the back of the corridor, away from the exit, but I had a plan.

"Stand back," I said, focusing on my heart maiden soul and facing the warriors. "Drop your weapons and stand back. Let us pass and you won't be hurt."

"We have our orders," Tobbar said. Shit, it hurt to see how many of Artan's and Theron's warriors were betraying us.

"Which are?" Trina asked.

"Capture the heart maiden alive, even if that means killing anyone else with her," he said. "Or dying in the process."

Shit.

"I don't want to hurt you." I pushed on the wall, and it advanced a couple of inches toward the warriors. Their eyes widened, but they held their ground. "And I certainly don't want to kill you." Or any more of them. "Please, let us go."

Tobbar shook his head. "I can't do that."

I let out a long, frustrating breath. "Then so be it."

I lifted my wall high and pushed against them. The warriors screamed as they retreated, trying to get away from the fire's path. The fire washed through the corridor like a big wave and then faded when it reached the stairs.

One warrior writhed on the ground, covered in third degree burns. A handful hid in the adjacent rooms, and the others had run up the stairs again—some of them had their hands or elbows or some random body part burned.

"Charge!" Tobbar cried.

The warriors came again. And again, I cast the fire wall and repeated the process.

"We'll be here forever at this rate," Trina muttered to me.

"I'm trying to scare them away," I told her.

"Well, it's not working." Her grip tightened around the hilt of her sword. "Drop the damn thing and let's take them out."

Shit.

After the second wave—and one more fallen warrior—I dropped the shield, and when Tobbar advanced on us, I didn't call it again.

Instead, Trina lifted her sword and fought with a couple, while I used fireballs to keep them away from me. Still reluctant to hurt them, I only packed enough power to make them unconscious, not to kill them.

I really didn't want to kill anyone else. Not today.

After what felt like an eternity, Trina and I cleared the corridor. Exhaustion had its claw around my muscles, but I pushed through and picked up Kane. Trina and I let out a string of curses as we went up the stairs, carrying him like a mummy.

By Saint Sara-la-Kali, if only he woke up ... even if I had to lend him a hand and help him walk, I bet it wouldn't be this heavy.

We were on the landing halfway through the second set of stairs when more footsteps rushed toward us.

"Fuck," Trina cursed. "I can't anymore."

I retreated a step, ready to put Kane down, when I felt

energy brushing against me and a familiar power trying to connect with my mind.

"Theron!"

He came down the stairs, followed by Artan, Cora, and Rye. He glanced at us, his eyes wide. "What happened?"

"Just ... take him," I told him.

Rye stepped forward and helped Theron with Kane. I sagged against the wall, suddenly too tired to even breathe properly.

"How did you find us?" Trina asked.

Theron jerked his chin to me. "We communicated last night. After that, I was able to follow the connection, even though it felt more like several puzzle pieces scattered everywhere, and here we are."

"What about the elder council?" I asked.

Artan cleared his throat. "They are busy."

I frowned. "What do you mean?"

"I lied to my *puri daj* about an emergency on the other side of the enclave," Artan said. I stared at him, perplexed. "But it won't take long for her and the other elders to figure out it was a lie."

"Let's go," Cora said, reaching for me. "Do you need help?"

I shook my head. "No, I think I can manage." A sudden rush of relief washed over me, and tears filled my eyes. If they had arrived a few minutes earlier, they would have seen the bodies of all the warriors I had stunned or killed, and for some reason, I really didn't want my friends to see that side of me. I didn't want them to know how unreliable and unstable I was right now. "Let's go."

We climbed the last set of stairs and crossed a doorway into the infirmary's supply room. I stared at the door, which apparently doubled as a shelf. I bet that if I entered the supply room and saw the shelf in its place, I would have never suspected there was a hidden opening behind it.

"It took me a while to figure out how to get to you," Theron said. "But when you contacted me, I just knew you were somewhere in the infirmary."

"Well, not in it, but under it."

He shrugged. "Potato, potato." He rested a heavy hand over my shoulder. "We have a car waiting. Let's go."

When we exited the infirmary, I was a little shocked to find out it was night. I didn't know why, since I had been so lost time wise. But in the end, it helped us while we sneaked through the enclave's streets, sticking to the shadows of the buildings, until we reached the main gate.

One of the Lovell vans waited for us, the engines on. Kizzy was behind the wheel, Felix had his nose glued to the window in the back, and Ellie rushed out and opened the door wide so Theron and Rye could put Kane inside.

I frowned. "What happened to the warriors guarding the gates?"

"There." Cora gestured to our right.

Leander and Lash approached us.

"Don't worry," Leander said, confident. "They will never know how you escaped."

My heart tugged. "But ..."

"But you should go," my mother said, walking from the other side of the van. Dolan was right beside her. "Get in that car and go."

I frowned. "Wait, do you mean you're not going?" Panic filled me. "But Darcy will know you helped me. She'll know you're on my side and she'll come for you."

My mother shook her head. "She won't. And if she comes, we'll be prepared."

Dolan put an arm over my mother's shoulder. My eyebrows shot up. "We'll protect each other."

"We'll be fine," my mother said. "Besides, you need someone on the inside. Sheila, Neil, and the two of us will be your eyes and ears."

I shook my head. It didn't make sense. I was running away, and they were staying? Why? We should all go and leave this enclave behind. A pang cut through my chest. I wasn't this heartless. Why was I considering this? There were plenty of innocent tziganes inside Lovell. I couldn't abandon them to Darcy and the elder council. I just had to make sure I lived another day before coming back and facing them.

I let out a long sigh. As if Damara and her gang weren't enough, I now had to worry about the elder council. Weren't they supposed to be fair and just and guide us through our problems and crises? To be honest, I didn't think they were evil, not in the way Damara was, but they weren't right either. And their methods were a tad bit violent.

Dolan pushed me toward the van. "Your friends are inside. Go before Sheila and Neil can't keep the elders busy anymore and they come this way."

Tears filled my eyes.

My mother hugged me. "We'll be fine. Just take care of yourself."

Dolan embraced me from the other side. "Be safe."

This was the first time I had ever been cocooned in my parents' arms, and I really liked it. Shame it couldn't last. I furiously wiped at my eyes, but one stubborn tears escaped. I kissed them both on the cheek, then hopped in the van.

Artan, who had taken the wheel back from Kizzy, glanced

to the backseat, where I was squeezed between Ellie and Theron. "Ready?"

I brushed a hand over my eyes again and sucked in a sharp breath. "Ready."

He peeled away from the enclave, the tires screeching on the pavement.

I looked back at my parents as Leander and Lash closed the gates.

I made a promise to myself. I would recover, I would fix the problem with the dying land, and then I would come back to bring the elder council down.

"I swear, no one will be there," Ellie said as she reached over the seat and entered the address in the van's GPS. "My parents only go to the mountain cabin for Thanksgiving, and the week between Christmas and New Year." She sat back, brushing her arm on mine. "Honestly, I don't even know why we have that cabin if we rarely use it."

"But it's a cabin, where will all of us sleep?" Theron asked.

"Well," Ellie started. "It has three bedrooms, but both living room sofas open into beds, and as far as I know, there are air mattresses and blankets in the closets."

"All right, everyone, sit tight," Artan said. "We're going to Ellie's mountain cabin, and it'll take us about two hours to get there."

I couldn't hold still anymore. I ended up unbuckling my seat belt and scooting to the second to last seat, where Kane was lying down. The guys had hastily tied two seat belts around him, so he wouldn't fall, but I undid them. Careful with my movements, I lifted his head and sat down. Then, I laid his head in my lap and stared at Kane's beautiful sleeping face, wishing he would wake up already.

"Why aren't you waking up, damn it," I whispered, afraid I was losing him.

About one hour on the road, Ellie was able to convince Artan to stop at a small grocery store, so we could buy supplies for the mountain cabin. After all, there hadn't been anyone there in a couple of months, and even if we stayed there a night, we would need food, beverages, and even toilet paper. After a quick stop and too many shopping bags, we resumed the trip up the mountain.

Once we arrived at the cabin, everyone helped with the shopping bags, our duffel bags—apparently, Ellie had packed for me before they put the plan into action—and with Kane. Theron embraced his chest and Rye grabbed his legs and they carted him inside. I stayed outside for a minute, trying to get used to all the changes that had occurred in such a short time.

Artan and Kizzy were married. The elder council had imprisoned and tortured Kane, Trina, and me. I had let the madness dip its fingers into my mind. I had killed our warriors during the escape. Kane had been unconscious for Saint Sara-la-Kali knew how long. And we were now fugitives from our own enclave.

Did I miss anything else?

Felix nudged his nose against my waist and I reached over, running my hand over his soft mane.

"I keep messing up, don't I?" He projected his feeling toward me, and I could feel his negation loud and clear. I chuckled, but it lacked sincerity. "Liar." With his mind, he told me he would stay outside, keeping guard. "I'll bring something for you to eat later, okay?" He blinked, and I could have sworn that was his way of saying yes.

Holding my breath, I joined the group inside the cabin. They were busy, assigning beds and organizing the groceries in the kitchen. Since I didn't see Kane on the couches, I assumed he was taken into one of the bedrooms and quietly tiptoed toward that side of the cabin.

I found him in the first suite, on a full bed in the middle of the room. I almost chuckled at how big he was for that bed, but a lump rose in my throat and tears filled my eyes again.

By Saint Sara-la-Kali, it seemed like all I ever did was cry now. I was tired of it.

Brushing away my unshed tears, I sat at the edge of the bed and traced my fingertips over Kane's face. "Please, wake up." I heard footsteps approaching, and for some reason, I knew who halted by the door. "I wish we could take him to a hospital."

"We can't," Trina said. "If we go, we'll be found out."

That was why I had said I wished ... "Then what do we do?"

"Other than the bruises, he isn't physically ill." She approached the bed. "This is magic from a potion."

I glanced at her. "Did you see them giving him a potion?"

She nodded. "Yes."

"So ... is there a way to undo it? Some sort of magic?" I stood and faced her. "Or maybe an antidote."

She pressed her lips together. "I think I can make one." She handed me a small piece of paper. "I already took note of everything I need to make him an antidote."

I looked up at the list. "Lots of herbs."

"Yes, and most of them can be found in the mountains."

My eyes widened. "I'll go right now."

She frowned. "I'm not stopping you, but it's in the middle of the night. It'll be hard to see anything."

I raised my hand and spark of fire crackled from it. "I can make light." I held the paper close to my chest. "You know nothing will stop me from getting the ingredients."

She nodded. "I know."

I glanced at Kane. Like this, he looked like he was sleeping. "Will you watch over him until I come back?"

"Trina will probably be busy, getting everything ready for the potion." Ellie stepped into the room and I stared at her, my eyes wide. "Sorry, I didn't mean to eavesdrop. I was heading to my bedroom when I heard you two." She placed a hand on my arm. "Go, find the herbs. I'll stay here."

I clutched her hand and squeezed it tight. "Thank you."

She nodded and practically pushed me out of the bedroom.

I walked past Cora as she found a bedroom, and paused at the kitchen, where Kizzy was preparing something. I turned to the front door, careful with my steps so she wouldn't notice me. A board creaked under my foot.

"Mirella!" Kizzy called. "Where are you going?"

Shit. "I need to go find something."

"First you need to eat." She spread jelly over a slice of bread. "I'm making you a couple of peanut butter and jelly sandwiches." She froze. "Do you like those? Please, tell me you like them." She looked down at the other two plates. "Damn it, what if you three don't like peanut butter and jelly."

"Three?" I asked, curious.

"Yeah, well ..." She grimaced. "Trina, Kane, and you have been locked away for a couple of days. Only Saint Sara-la-Kali knows if you ate anything while down there. I thought you could be hungry." She sighed. "I should have asked what you wanted first, shouldn't I?"

"Hm …" I didn't know what to say. It was the middle of the night, and despite being hungry, food was the last thing on my mind. Right now, all I wanted was to find the damn herbs and wake up Kane. "You know, Kane is in some kind of coma, so he won't be eating until we can wake him."

"Right," she muttered.

"And I'm in a rush. I'll eat when I get back, okay?" I really didn't want to tell her that I loved peanut butter, but not jelly. "You can see if Trina is up for it, though."

"Sure."

I pretended not to hear the disappointment in her voice. Better that way.

I opened the door and a new thought came to mind. "Where are the guys?"

"Artan, Rye, and Theron went out to check the perimeter," she said, her eyes downcast. "They wanted to make sure we weren't followed."

"Good." I hated watching Kizzy spread the jelly on the bread, as if she were stabbing it. I really had hurt her feelings. "Hm, just … give me one with peanut butter, please."

She beamed. "Of course." In less than a minute, Kizzy handed me a sandwich. "Here you go."

I took a big bite. "Thanks," I said, my mouth half full. "I'll eat it while I work."

Without waiting for more questions or comments, I fled the cabin, afraid that she would make me sit down and talk to her while I ate. I didn't have time to waste. Although, I had to confess, eating something helped with the exhaustion that crawled over every inch of my body.

When I got back to the cabin, I would make another sandwich for myself.

I conjured a bright flame over my open palm and trudged ahead. The faster I found the herbs, the faster Trina could make the potion and Kane would be awake.

Hopefully.

I couldn't let any negative thoughts in my mind right now. I had to be optimistic. I would find all the herbs, and Kane would wake up in no time. I was sure of it.

But uncertainty and fear wrapped around my heart. I felt like it would suffocate me if I didn't push it back, and—

I let out a yelp when a whoosh of air pushed my hair back and almost put out my flame.

Artan landed in front of me. He used to do that a lot last fall. I should have known he would be patrolling the area from above and wouldn't miss an opportunity to scare me.

"Where are you going?" he asked, all business.

I increased the power of my flame. "I need to find some herbs."

A frown appeared between his brows. "At this time of night?"

"It's time sensitive." I was sure my feelings for him were resolved. Besides bittersweet memories and a little sadness about how things had progressed between the two of us, I really didn't harbor any other feeling for him. And yet, I found myself getting irritated easily and wanting to escape him. "Excuse me." I walked around him.

"Mirella." He reached for me.

I stepped to the side. "What are you doing?"

"I just don't think you should go out there alone."

I always hated when he acted macho. And now that he

was married to another woman, did he really think he could control me?

"I'll be fine," I told him as I resumed my trek.

"Mirella, wait." I shouldn't have stopped, but I did. I didn't turn though. I heard his long exhale. "I'm sorry ... for everything." Did he want me to say something to that? I wouldn't. "And thank you for being a good friend to Kizzy."

Did she really consider me a friend? I sometimes thought she tried to keep me close so she would know what I was doing, so she would know if I tried to get to Artan. Could she really just be a nice girl and want to be friends?

I had my doubts.

Without another word, I let go of my flame, enveloping myself in darkness, and marched into the mountains.

It didn't take long to find all the herbs Trina had asked. When I got back to the cabin, Felix was seated in front of the door, like a good attack cat. Inside, most people were sleeping, except Trina, Theron, and Ellie. Theron constantly looked out the windows, expecting an attack; Ellie watched over Kane; and Trina had gotten a big pot from the kitchen and had started what she could for the potion.

According to Ellie, Kane hadn't moved or breathed differently. Which was good and bad. Good because he wasn't getting worse. But bad because I wished he would wake up already!

Trying to occupy my mind with something else, I helped Trina with the potion in the kitchen. She handed me a cutting board she had found underneath the sink, and I began chopping the herbs as she had instructed me to do.

Talking would help my anxious mind, so I asked, "Will you tell me how you learned alchemy?"

She inhaled deeply. "My father was an alchemist."

"What?" That ... I wasn't expecting that.

"Yeah, I'm only half tzigane," she said with a hollow chuckle. "My father kidnapped my mother. She was a tzigane and he wanted her blood, but for some reason, he couldn't do it. And in the span of a few days, he fell in love with her." She paused. "And she fell in love with him."

"Hm, what happened, then?"

"In the end, he let her go. She wanted to run away with him, but he said they would never be free. Alchemists would hunt them both, and they would never have peace. So, my mother went back to the enclave, where she soon learned she was pregnant."

"And she was pushed away because of that?" I asked, sure she would say yes. That was what had happened to my mother when she got pregnant with me.

But Trina shook her head, surprising me. "No. My mother was already promised to a tzigane, and he was very much in love with her. She told him she was pregnant, and all he did was hurry up their wedding so they could lie that the baby was his."

I gasped, shocked, but content with the guy's decision. "Wait. But ... how do you know? They told you?"

"They didn't have a choice." She stopped mixing the ingredients and looked at me. "My father came for me."

"What?" I almost yelled, but was able to remember it was the middle of the night and most people in the cabin were asleep. "What happened?"

"I was about fourteen years old, I think, when he approached my mother, saying he had left the alchemists a couple of years ago and had been hiding. He wanted to try it alone to see if he could escape the alchemists for real before calling her and taking her with him. But he didn't know she had already married and had had a kid. Of course, he ended up finding out I was his." She paused. "He was hurt my mother had another man and hadn't told him about me, but then he asked for me to come with him. At the time, I was a rebellious teenager and I was insanely mad that my mother and my father— stepfather—had lied to me about my real father. So, despite my mother's protests and attempts to lock me inside the house, I left with him."

My curiosity only grew. "And?"

She got a bunch of the herbs I had chopped and put them in the pot. "At first, we lived in hiding while he taught me alchemy. But it was hard. Since I was living as a tzigane and had no interest in being an alchemist, I wanted to live as a human, but someone like me out in the open? It was a beacon for all kinds of creatures."

"I know that well," I muttered, remembering the days when I didn't know what I was. My mother and I moved a lot, and when I looked back, I could see that she had tried to lead a quiet life with me, as if she were hiding.

"After a couple of years rebelling and causing trouble, I ended up back at the enclave with my mother and stepfa- ther." She extended her hand over the pot and cut her palm with a kitchen knife. I gasped, surprised, but soon remem- bered what she once had told me. Alchemists' potions only worked with tzigane blood. The potion hissed and Trina stirred it faster. "Thankfully, they hadn't told the truth about me to the *rom baro* and elders of our enclave. They said I had gone to spend some time with relatives at another enclave. That seemed to appease them."

"What about your father? The real one?" I asked.

She shrugged. "I don't know. Never saw or heard from him again."

"I'm so—"

"It's ready," she announced, cutting me off. I watched her as she put some of the potion in a glass using a ladle. I knew what she was doing. Closing off, avoiding sympathy, and putting on a brave facade. It didn't make me any less sorry for what she had went through, though. Trina handed me the glass. "Here. Make sure he drinks it all, even if it's a little bit now, so he won't choke on it, then the rest when he comes to."

I took the glass from her, too eager. "Thank you."

I rushed to the bedroom and found Ellie seated in a chair beside the table, her eyes closed, her head fallen to her chest. My poor friend had stayed up while the others slept to help me. I was thankful for her.

Gently, I put a hand on her shoulder and shook her.

She blinked "What? What?" She saw me there. "I wasn't sleeping."

I chuckled. "Right."

"No, seriously. I was just resting my eyes." She saw the glass in my hand. "Is that ...?"

I nodded. "The potion."

Ellie stood and pushed the chair back, giving me space to approach Kane. She helped me put another pillow underneath his head, then she stood by my side, biting her nails.

Holding my breath, I poured a couple of drops of the potion in Kane's mouth. I waited. Nothing happened.

"Try again," Ellie said.

"He's supposed to drink all of this," I told her.

She made a huge O with her mouth.

Again, I dropped a little of the potion past Kane's lips.

Afraid of pouring the entire thing down his throat and choking him, I repeated the gesture every ten seconds. By the time he had drank half of the glass and still hadn't moved, I started getting nervous.

"Is Trina sure this will wake him up?" Ellie asked.

I glanced at the glass. Was Trina sure? I didn't know anymore. She had said she knew a potion, but I didn't remember if she had promised it would work. "I don't know," I confessed. "But it's the only thing we've got."

I tipped the glass to pour a little more of the potion in Kane's mouth when a hand shot up and held my wrist.

"Put any more of that in my mouth and I might throw up."

I gasped and almost dropped the glass. "Kane!"

Groaning, he reached up and rubbed his eyes. "By Saint Sara-la-Kali, my head hurts." He scooted to his elbows and tried to get up. "Fuck, no, everything hurts." He laid back down.

I dropped the glass on the nightstand and cupped his face. "Are you okay? What are you feeling? Is anything hurting? What—?"

A small chuckle rumbled in his chest, and it turned into a groan. "Calm down, Mirella, before—" He gasped and sat up, looking around. "What happened? Where are we?" He reached for me, clasping my arms tight, and looked me over. "Are you okay? How did you escape? How did *we* escape?"

Slipping my hands into his, I sat beside him and told him all that had happened since we were separated, starting with how I had had an episode in front of Darcy and other council members.

At some point in the story, Ellie stepped out of the room and closed the door behind her. Hopefully, she went to rest. We all needed rest, including Kane.

"You're probably still weak." I handed him the glass. "You have to drink this."

"Fuck, no," he grumbled. "That tastes horrible."

"And yet, it's what woke you up. You have to drink the rest, though."

Glaring at the glass, Kane drank the potion. A shudder rolled down his body. "Shit, that was nasty."

I pushed him down on the bed. "You're not well yet. Get some sleep."

He groaned again. "I'm definitely not one hundred percent, but I'm not sleepy." He pulled me and I fell in bed beside him. His arms wrapped around me and he held me close. I worried I was pressing against one of his wounds, but when he started talking, I forgot about that. "I was worried I wouldn't see you again. When they took me, and later, during one of my torture session, they told me they had taken you too. I tried so hard to break free, but the most I did was escape the cell. After that, the torture sessions only got harder."

I buried my nose in the crook of his neck and inhaled deeply. His vetiver and musk scent filled my nose and my mind, and I was so relieved he was here with me. "We're together now. We're okay."

He kissed the top of my head. "Any plans about what we're going to do now?"

"Not really, though I know what I want to do tomorrow morning."

"And what is that?"

I pulled back a little so I could look into his eyes. "I'm going to tell everyone about the fire heart fever."

10

Kane didn't sleep, but I ended up dozing off for a couple of hours in his arms. Or so I thought. When I finally woke up, it was midafternoon.

"Why did you let me sleep so long?" I asked Kane, as I got ready for a much needed shower. After my days locked in the hospital-like room without a proper bath, I was feeling like I couldn't be near myself.

He ran a hand through his damp hair. He too had spent many days without cleaning up, but now he looked sharp with a five o'clock shadow and his fresh clothes. "I had been out for a long time and got some rest that way. As far as I know, you haven't slept well in days, and you were weakened by the tort—" He pressed his lips tight, not wanting to say the word.

Torture.

I knew how simply thinking about that hurt. I couldn't bear thinking about how he had been tortured, especially with magic, and how bad it had gone that they had to force feed him a potion and he had fallen into a magical coma. Although the methods had been different, we both suffered. And we had suffered for each other.

After a long shower, Kane and I joined the others in the living room-breakfast-kitchen combo of the cabin. Last night, I had been in such a rush and focused on working on the potion, I hadn't paid attention to the place, but now that I took a good look at it, it was cozy and warm. That was what I thought when I saw the wooden walls, the stone fireplace that took over an entire wall, and the window panels that took up another. The view was the stunning green of the mountainside, and above it the blue skies and the bright sun.

It was a beautiful day.

"Are you hungry?" Ellie asked, showing me a pot. "We made some alfredo pasta, if you want some."

At that, my stomach growled. I had eaten two peanut butter sandwiches last night, but before that ... I didn't know. I didn't recall when I had last been fed while I was being held by the council.

But that would have to wait as something had been building inside my chest since last night, a pressure that would hurt and burst if I didn't get it out soon. "Later," I said, halting behind one of the armchairs. I didn't think I could sit down for this. "First, I need to tell you all something."

All eyes turned to me.

"What is it?" Theron asked, his tone soft, like a real concerned brother. After the long period he had barely looked my way, his worry was enough to make me cry.

I inhaled deeply. "I bet you're all wondering what happened that day at the festival." They had seen as pain had assaulted me and hallucinations had taken over, so strong they had made me pass out. "It's the *Yog Ozi Nas*. The fire heart fever."

"What?" Cora asked.

"I've never heard of it," Rye said.

Artan frowned. "What is that?"

Kane stood by my side, like a strong pillar. Good thing too, because I was suddenly nervous about revealing the truth to my friends.

"When the heart maiden acquires the heart flower, a lot of its power stays with the heart maiden," I started. "This accumulated power is too strong, and with time, it can bring on pain and hallucinations and eventually drive a heart maiden crazy. The illness is called the fire heart fever." I paused. "And that's what you saw happening that morning at the festival site." I glanced at Kane and he nodded at me. "For some reason, when Kane is near me, I don't feel anything. But that day, he had been dragged away, and I think my desperation to help him, plus his increasing distance, brought forward the fire heart fever symptoms."

Artan crossed his arms. Kizzy pressed a hand to her chest. Ellie gasped. As expected, they were shocked and I hadn't even told them everything.

"But ... what does that mean?" Cora asked. "You're going crazy?"

I nodded. "The fire heart fever is strong already, and now the elder council knows it."

"So now they can help you, right?" Ellie asked. "I mean, they are the enclave's authority. They want the well-being of all tziganes. Right?"

"Didn't you just see how they dragged her away and tortured her?" Theron asked, a bite to his words.

"Yeah," Ellie muttered, shrinking into herself. "I guess I

hoped it had been a fluke. That something else had happened and it hadn't been the council."

"It was the elder council," Kane said, plain and simple. "They were the ones who tortured Mirella, Trina, and me."

"I knew something was wrong, but that can't be." Artan paced in front of the fireplace. "It can't be. My *puri daj*, my *dat* ... they aren't this evil. They can't be."

"They are," Trina retorted. "They truly are."

"I don't believe they are evil," I said. Everyone turned to me like I had gone crazy. Well, I had just told them that was true. "I would like to believe they are misguided and have lost their way along the years. Plus, I doubt the current elder council had ever considered they would have a new heart maiden to take care of themselves." With almost two hundred years without any heart maiden, they had grown lax. "But because of me, they suddenly had to follow all the rules that had been used centuries before."

"And that means incarcerating you?" Cora asked, appalled.

I pressed my lips tight.

"Tell them," Kane said, his voice low. "You said you were going to tell them all of it."

"There's more?" Rye asked.

Kane dipped his chin once. "A lot more."

Artan muttered curse words.

I braced myself for the rest of the story. "They aren't only supposed to lock a heart maiden away and try to control her. They can't. The heart maiden will only grow stronger and the madness will take over. Damara guided me—"

"Damara?" Artan asked, his eyes wide.

"Yes, since the fire heart fever began, she can enter my

mind," I admitted. "I can keep her away most of the time, but when I have an episode … I have no control over my mind."

"That's great," he muttered.

I swear I wanted to kick him right now. Instead, I closed my eyes for a moment and continued my tale. "Damara guided me to a secret room in the library where the heart maiden records are hidden." Again, they all looked at me, too shocked to believe me. "Before, when they tried to allow the heart maiden to continue her duties, most of them went completely mad, as in nobody-can-control-her mad. They ended up committing atrocities, like killing their own families." Gasps and curses filled the room. "So, when the heart maiden showed signs she was reaching an irreversible point, the elder council would kill her."

"What?"

"I don't think I heard you right."

"It can't be."

"They wouldn't do that."

Could I scare them anymore than this? If it weren't tragic, it would be hilarious. I took in a sharp breath. "The elder council creates a situation and makes it look like an accident. I've read records of the heart maidens who have died while fighting alchemists or revenants, and many other cases, but in truth, they have all been killed by the council at a young age." I swallowed hard. "Now that they know I have the fire heart fever, they will kill me soon."

"But you just said Kane can stop the symptoms," Kizzy said.

"Yeah, how is that possible?" Trina asked.

"We don't know," Kane said. "All we know is that if she's away from me, the symptoms come back."

"How far away?" Theron asked.

"We aren't sure," I said. "Once, at Kane's mountain house, I was three miles away, I think. The last time during the festival, I think I was less than that, but like I said before, I think the situation didn't help and I snapped."

"So, you're fine now?" Ellie asked, worried. "You're okay, right, because Kane is right beside you."

Kane put an arm over my shoulders and pulled me to him. "She's fine."

I groaned. "It depends on how you define fine."

Kane tensed beside me. "What do you mean?"

"I ... I didn't know what else to do while I was locked away and being tortured, so I kind of welcomed the madness." I wanted to recoil into myself. "That was how I reached Theron's mind and escaped my room and freed Trina and Kane." I paused and tears brimmed in my eyes. "And burned a dozen of warriors alive.

Trina averted her eyes. She had seen the bodies firsthand.

"What happened?" Kane asked, his voice gentle.

I shrugged, completely ashamed. "I think I just lost it. I was so deep in the madness, I didn't know what I was doing. I only came back myself again when I saw you in the cell, unresponsive."

"So Kane saved you again," Ellie said with a small smile. How could she smile at me right now? "He's like your guardian angel."

Kizzy sighed. "That's so romantic."

Artan groaned beside her.

Theron frowned. "But you're fine now, right?"

"I don't know," I confessed. "Since finding Kane and Trina and then escaping with you all, I haven't had any episodes, if that's what you're asking. I haven't felt the madness trying to take over." I stepped away from Kane. His arm dropped. "But

... I'm scared. I'm scared the madness will come now regardless of what I do to keep it away, and I'm going to end up hurting you guys. I can't bear it if I hurt any of you." My voice broke at the last word.

Arms open, Ellie rushed to me. "Don't worry about that."

Then Kizzy was embracing me too. "It wasn't your fault."

How could they say that? How could they touch me when I could burn them in less than a second?

I tried pushing them away, but then Theron approached and put his arms around me too.

"We're here for you," he whispered.

Then, Rye and Cora reached over and put their hands on my shoulders. Then it was Trina's turn. Artan hesitated, but he placed his hand on Kizzy's back, as if he could transfer me his intention through her. Well, with our history, I would accept that.

From our mountain of arms and heads, I glanced at Kane. He stood a couple of feet from us all, a smile on his lips. I reached over between the bodies around me, and he grasped my hand, squeezing it tight.

For the first time in a long time, I felt strong, I felt whole, and I felt loved.

And that was all I need to be ready to declare war.

***

AFTER A LATE LUNCH, I WENT OUT TO CHECK ON FELIX. I brought him a piece of steak, but he was lying in the grass, the remains of a rabbit in his mouth.

I averted my eyes and gagged.

"Here." I tossed the piece of steak to him before I truly barfed. "Enjoy this too." He projected an image of me seated beside him and him with his big, heavy head in my lap. I scrunched my nose. "Sorry, buddy, I can't do that today." Not with the blood and flesh all over his mouth. "But I'll do this." I stepped closer and scratched the back of his head—like this, the top of his head came to my chest. "Anything to report?" I asked, as if he would actually tell me if he saw anything suspicious in the forest. But all I saw in my mind were images of quiet trees and a couple of critters.

"Why did you never tell me?"

I froze. Slowly, I turned around and found Artan at the edge of the cabin's porch, about five feet from me. I shrugged. "Things were already complicated between us when the symptoms started."

"But if I had known—"

"You would have pushed me away faster," I said, my tone firm. "Or told your grandmother, who would have locked me away sooner."

His brows slammed down. "I wouldn't have told her."

I admit that was a low blow. "Maybe not, but you were already looking at me in a funny way. The distance between us was only growing. I didn't feel like putting another nail in the coffin." I hugged myself. "I didn't want to tell anyone about it, to be honest. I was afraid of their reaction if they knew I was losing it."

"But you told Kane."

Why did he have to act like a jealous prick? I lifted my index finger. "One, you're married. Back then, you were engaged. You shouldn't be this upset about it." I lifted my middle finger. "Two, I didn't tell Kane. He found out."

"Still—"

"Okay, stop right there." He was irritating me again, and I was so done with his bullshit. "If you need to know, yes, Kane and I are together, and I've never been happier. Now, back off. You should worry about your wife." I jerked my chin to the window behind him.

Artan turned and met Kizzy's eyes. The poor thing looked sad seeing her husband talking to his ex. "By Saint Sara-la-Kali."

"Whatever problems arise between you two, know I don't want any part of it." I patted Felix's head once more and walked past Artan. "Try to be happy with her, please. For everyone's sake."

I entered the house and Kizzy busied herself with fluffing the couch pillows. I paused, wanting to tell her she had nothing to worry about, but I didn't think that would help right now.

Instead, I went to the kitchen, where Ellie and Theron were starting our dinner, and grabbed a glass of water.

"I want to help," I told them.

"Nah, it's fine," Ellie said, smiling. "We have it under control."

I stared at my best friend, hoping she understood the meaning in my eyes. "Please, just give me something to do."

Her smile slipped away. "Sure." She handed me a bowl with potatoes. "You asked for it."

Groaning, I grabbed the bowl and the peeler and sat at the dining table to work.

WE TOOK THE REST OF THE DAY OFF, TRYING TO REST AND GET ready for what was to come later. And that was the subject we discussed while having dinner that night.

Although we didn't know exactly which steps to take, we

all agreed on three things: One, we should leave the cabin the next morning, because we had stayed here for too long already. Two, we had to find a way to fix the error I made during the spring festival ceremony and undo the spreading darkness. And three, we had to find a way to cure the fire heart fever.

"Let's just take it easy tonight," Theron spoke up. Since Artan had started acting like a jerk and left the enclave two months ago, he had assumed the leadership position in our group, and I doubted he wanted to hand it back. Honestly, I didn't want it either. "Let's think about where to go next and any ideas about the failed ceremony and cures for the fire heart disease. Tomorrow morning, we'll hash out a plan before we leave."

After dinner, we quieted down, and after a round of tea, everyone went to bed. Kane and I had one bedroom for the two of us, and even though I would have to do more, both of us were still hurt, and with purple wounds from the torture sessions. So, we just snuggled and fell asleep.

But, in the middle of night, I woke up with my throat dry. After successfully disentangling myself from Kane, I tiptoed to the kitchen where I got a glass of water.

I heard a low growl and looked out the window. Felix was standing there, his eyes on mine. I opened my mind to him and he projected an image of Trina sneaking out of the house.

"What the ...?"

I glanced at the clock on the wall. It was almost five in the morning. As far as I knew, Trina had been assigned night duty right now. In about an hour, Rye was supposed to replace her.

I set the glass down and went outside.

"Which direction did she go?" I asked Felix. He jumped off the porch and went to the closest tree line. He let out a low yelp. "Thanks," I said, walking past him. I patted his head, before following the direction.

Where the hell had Trina gone?

11

FOR SOME REASON, I DIDN'T CALL ON MY FIRE TO ILLUMINATE the way as I weaved through the forest—at least the moon was bright enough for me to not trip on my feet—and I didn't try to call Trina's name. I just went in the direction Felix had told me to, and followed the trail, my instinct as my guide.

It didn't take long for me to find her.

She slowed down and soon stopped all together.

And I stayed behind a few trees, observing her.

Trina knelt beside a creek and opened a small leather pouch. She grabbed a handful of whatever powder was inside and spread it over the edge of the water. A round halo, like the frame of mirror, appeared on the water's surface, shining a bright golden light.

Then she began talking.

I couldn't make out her words, much less her sentences, but I knew she was talking to someone through that magical portal thing.

What the hell was she up to?

Just as I made up my mind to reveal myself and see who

she was talking to, Trina put her hand in the water and waved back and forth. The bright light and the halo were gone.

Tying the leather pouch to her waist, Trina shot up. She glanced from side to side, and I hid behind the tree before taking off.

I muttered a curse and rushed after her.

The dark feeling that something was wrong only grew inside me as I followed her through the forest. What was she doing? What was Trina hiding?

Intent on confronting her, I sped up.

But Trina had caught on that someone was following her. She paused before turning a sharp left and disappearing behind a thick patch of trees. I ran after her, but a couple of minutes later, it was obvious that I had lost her.

By Saint Sara-la-Kali.

With a heavy sigh, I started my way back to the cabin.

It was only then that it hit me. I had purposely left the cabin and Kane behind. What if Trina had gone more than three miles from the cabin? Then the fire heart fever would have hit me, and I could be in trouble right now. Following Trina like that had been stupid. As usual, I didn't think through the consequences before following my instincts. I really had to learn to stop doing that.

I was ninety percent sure I was going the right away— what if I was going the wrong way? I would end up farther away from Kane—when the air changed and goose bumps crawled up my arms.

My steps faltered and I opened up my senses, trying to find the source of such change.

My senses went out in a circle, widening as it went farther from me. I felt the plants, the critters, the bugs ...

And revenants.

There were over two dozen revenants a few yards behind me.

Panic gripped my chest. I sped up my steps and pulled back my senses. Trying to stay calm, I reached my mind toward Theron's. My damn half-brother was sleeping, but I pushed through until I shouted inside his skull.

Revenants!

He jerked awake. *What?*

Revenants. Somewhere outside the cabin. Felix knows where. Find me!

On my way!

Screeches echoed through the air. Apparently, the revenants weren't hiding anymore. They were in full on chasing mode.

I ran faster, praying I didn't trip and fall on my face. Praying I made it back to my friends before the revenants got to me. Praying that ten against thirty revenants was enough.

Soon, a voice rang through the trees.

"Mirella!" Kane shouted.

I turned in his direction. "Here!"

A moment later, I ran smack into his chest. He wrapped his arms around me. "Are you all right?" He pulled back and examined my face. "Are you hurt?"

"I'm fine." I glanced over my shoulder. "But you should move *now*, before they get to us."

"Later, we'll talk about this night outing without me." He sounded hurt. "Right now, get ready to fight." He tugged me to his side and drew out his twin swords. "The others are two steps behind."

I stared at him, my eyes wide. In the back of my mind, I had known we would have to fight these revenants no matter what. Even if I had made it back to the cabin, the revenants wouldn't have stopped. They would have attacked and destroyed the cabin in the process.

"There you are!" Theron said, joining us.

He looked terrible with his long hair messed up, and his uniform barely tightened. In fact, as the others joined us and we formed a line to receive the revenants, I realized they all seemed like they had fell out of bed into their clothes, grabbed the first weapons they could reach, and ran into the wind. All but Felix, who always had his mane sticking in all directions.

To my surprise, Trina joined the line. She pulled out her sword and fell into a fighting stance. "What do we have here?"

I stared at her, shocked that she was acting like she hadn't just sneaked out and talked to someone using alchemy. I opened my mouth to call her out, but Artan cut me off.

"Revenants," he hissed as the first of the vampire-like creatures stepped through the trees and faced us.

"I count ten," Rye said. "We'll finish this quickly."

I shook my head. "Try at least three times that."

"What?" Cora almost shrieked.

The rest of the revenants stepped forward from the shadows.

I glanced around. The revenants had spread out.

We were surrounded.

12

THE REVENANTS DIDN'T WASTE TIME. THEY LUNGED AT US, their sharp teeth bared, their claws out.

Kane swept his swords wide, grazing his blade across the chest of a revenant, but he let out a long groan as he clutched his shoulder. He was still hurt from the torture, still weak.

A protective feeling inundated me, and I channeled my power.

These revenants would be sorry for having disturbed our night.

The heat of my fire filled my veins, burning me up. When the next revenant made his move, I threw out my hands and let my fire out. A thick jet of fire flew from my hands and enveloped the revenant. It screamed as my fire burned it alive, and soon, it was shuddering on the ground, my fire gone, its body a black, charred mass.

I took in a deep breath as my muscles protested. Truth was, I hadn't recovered from my days locked away either. And if Trina was feeling like Kane and me, then it meant only seven out of ten were really fighting. Well, maybe only six if I counted Ellie. She didn't have any magic or possess any real combat training. Theron had taught her some self-defense moves, but that was it. She could not fight an entire throng of revenants with self-defense.

Two revenants came for Kane and me. I grabbed his hand and tugged him back, falling behind a tree. Then, I torched the revenants like the previous one. When I was done, I leaned against the tree beside Kane and took in a long breath.

"You're tired," he said. "Scale down on your magic, or you'll crash."

I knew he was right, but this was the only way for me to kill them. "We can finish this soon. And if I crash later, you just let me nap." I winked at him.

Shaking his head, Kane stepped to the side, facing an incoming revenant. He dodged its attack and ran his blades clean through the vampire's neck, cutting its head off.

I looked around. Because of our location in the forest—in the middle of thick trees—we were separated and we didn't have much room to move. The ones handling swords could barely use them, in fear of hitting the person next to them, or driving the swords into tree trunks.

We had to retreat to a clearing, or this would take forever.

A revenant jumped from above the tree right in front of me. Surprised, it took me a moment to react. I channeled my power, but by then, the revenant already had its claws around my neck. It pushed me against the tree as it squeezed my throat. It hissed, leaning into me and showing its razor-sharp teeth. Its foul odor reached my nostril and I gagged.

"Mirella!" Kane shouted, but he was too busy fending off other two revenants.

I had been in worse situations before. I shoved my hands into the creature's chest and called on my magic. Fire burned in my hands and spread through the revenant's body. Shrieking, it let go of me. Fire consumed its body. I sidestepped as it fell toward me.

"Take the heart maiden," a voice boomed. "Kill the rest."

I glanced in the voice's direction and saw a red alchemist standing behind the bulk of the revenants. These weren't random revenants. They were here by Damara's orders.

And they wanted me.

I couldn't let my friends get hurt because of me. I had to end this fight soon, because this was a battle, not the war. If we lost here, we wouldn't win later.

I channeled my power, intent on creating a huge fire that wiped out the damn revenants, and hopefully the red alchemist too.

Theron broke through the revenants and jumped the red alchemists. The shadow sword appeared in the alchemist's hand, but he was no match for Theron. Three moves later, the red alchemist was on the ground.

The revenants let out a low hiss, probably passing along some kind of information, or order.

And, from the enraged glint in their dark eyes, the order was to attack.

I raised my hands, sending my fire out.

The revenants retreated. At first, I thought they were running from my fire, but I soon realized all of them were running, not just the ones I had attacked.

I reined in my fire and glanced around. "What's going on?"

"They are just leaving," Cora said, her breathing ragged. Apparently, Kane and I weren't the only ones exhausted here.

"But why?" Rye asked.

Kane glanced to all sides. "It doesn't make sense."

Trina stilled beside us. "Shh. I hear something."

We all fell silent and listened. At first, there was nothing. Just the low whistle of the ruffling wind, or the chirp of bugs as the night fell away.

Then, we heard it.

Howls.

And they were getting closer.

"Run!" Artan shouted.

Kane clasped my hand and ran, pulling me with him. My friends and I darted toward the cabin, while Felix waited a few seconds, taking our backs. If these howls were really wolves, could he stop them? I would rather he ran with us.

I skidded to a stop to call him.

Like a rolling wave, the wolves dotted the forest, descending on us.

My stomach dropped.

"Run faster!" Theron yelled at us all. He was holding on to Ellie, but her short legs couldn't keep up with him.

I lost my footing as I ran, speeding up as much as I could, but I also didn't have the long legs or the powerful muscles the guys had.

Running at my full speed was nothing for wolves.

One by one, the wolves jumped on our backs, pushing us to the ground. Kane went down one second before the air fled my lungs and I was thrown down by a giant wolf. Its weight pressed on me, making it hard to move.

A second wolf approached me. It sniffed my hair.

"Get away from her!" Kane shouted, his voice shaking with rage.

Slowly, the wolf shifted, transforming into a tall man with short blond hair. And naked. Completely naked. He knelt beside me and I closed my eyes, not eager to look at his junk.

Wait ... they were werewolves?

"Is she the one?" he asked someone behind me.

"I think so," someone else said. Another werewolf in human form, I was assuming. "What do we do with the rest?"

At that, I snapped my eyes open, no matter the view in front of me. "If it's me you're after, then you have to let the others go." I relaxed my muscles. "I'll go peacefully, just let the others go."

"Mirella!" Theron snapped.

"No!" Artan shouted.

"Over my dead body," Kane snarled.

"The truth is, we need to bring all of you," the first werewolf said. He stood up and looked around, as if this was a simple task he did every day. "Take them all."

The werewolf on top of me transformed into a human—naked again—and several other men stepped forward and held my arms. They hoisted me up.

I stared at the first werewolf. "What is going on? Where are you taking us?"

He offered me a knowing glance. "To our pack leader. He'll decide your fate."

13

———

THE WEREWOLVES TIED OUR WRISTS WITH SOME KIND OF magical rope, connecting us together in a long line, and escorted us down the opposite side of the mountain—most of them in their werewolf form, snapping their teeth at us each time we tripped or talked to each other.

Even Felix had been tied up and muzzled and was being practically dragged by our captors.

Any plans? I asked Theron.

Other than using our magic to break the rope and fighting them, no.

I glanced down at the ropes. *I already tried magic. Even my fire barely warms the rope. It won't break that easily.*

Besides, breaking the rope and fighting, we didn't have any options, and we were sorely outnumbered by these vicious creatures.

They seemed to know who you are, Theron said. *Which means, the alpha is after you.*

What could he possibly want with me?

I don't know, but I guess you'll have to reason with him and beg for our lives.

Would that work? This alpha could be as evil as Damara or Darcy. I was terribly afraid we were heading toward another enemy.

Eventually, the werewolves guided us toward a small cave opening.

"Through here," said the man from before. He had remained in his human body the entire trip.

I glanced at the cave. Kane and Theron couldn't get through walking side by side. They really expected us to willingly walk in there? What if they pushed us all in and then closed the exit, sealing us in.

I hesitated, but the ropes tugged me forward. "Move!" the man shouted.

Some of us uttered protests, but I knew my voice would add nothing to the mix. I had to hope this wasn't a trap. That we were being escorted to the alpha, like they said, and that the alpha was a compassionate werewolf.

So far, I had little indication of that.

We were pulled inside the cave, and I felt like I would suffocate as we were guided through a long, narrow, rocky tunnel. Finally, after a couple of minutes, the tunnel widened and the opens for other tunnels appeared.

We were taken down into the earth, until the tunnel suddenly ended in a vast cavern. I swear it was bigger than a football stadium, but with rocks for a ceiling. More cave openings lined the perimeter and several people and werewolves peaked out as we were escorted deeper into the room, all of them probably curious about the prisoners.

There were kids among them. Certainly, they wouldn't kill us in front of kids, right? I mean, I was praying they weren't that barbaric.

The few werewolves who were in their human forms picked up leather or suede pants from a wooden chest near the entrance and put them on, finally covering some of their naked bodies, before tugging on the ropes again.

Our group was pulled across the vast space, to stand in front of a raised platform with a big wooden log, covered with a piece of ragged leather.

What was this?

The werewolves surrounded us, ready to move if we moved first.

A man with the same leather pants as the others, but who also wore a realistic wolf mask covering his face, approached the platform and sat down on the log. The werewolves, in both forms, lowered their heads to him.

The alpha.

"You should bow too," the werewolf beside me muttered.

I hesitated. I didn't want to bow to anyone. What if he was evil? What if he was going to make my friends and I suffer? A person like that didn't deserve my respect.

On the other hand, I probably shouldn't defy him, not yet. Our well-being depended on his mercy, and if I started by being defiant, things would only go south.

Gritting my teeth, I lowered my head.

"Rise," the alpha said, his voice muffled by the mask. I looked up, trying to think of what to say next. How to beg for our lives, how to get out of here alive, but before I could manage to utter a word, he continued, "Cut the rope."

The werewolves turned to us, and with their claws, cut the rope around our wrists. I felt the magic being lifted as the ropes fell to the ground, useless now.

I rubbed at my reddened wrists. "W-what's going on?" I

managed to ask. Because honestly, if he had brought us here to kill us, he wouldn't set us free, would he?

Slowly, the alpha unfolded his long figure and took off his mask.

My heart stopped. Theron sucked in a sharp breath. The others gasped in shock.

I pressed my hands to my mouth and shook my head. "No."

"It can't be," Theron whispered.

Ramon smiled at us. "It's really me."

My brother, who we thought had perished, burned by my fire in the damn prison, stood tall and strong in front of us. Besides burn scars across his chest and arms, and longer, messier hair, he looked the same.

And he was the alpha of this pack.

Tears brimmed in my eyes. "I saw you die."

Ramon climbed down from the platform, and with arms open, walked toward us. I didn't think, I stepped into his embrace. A moment later, Theron bumped into us and wound his arms around Ramon too.

A long time passed and I still couldn't let go. Seven months ago, if someone told me I would cling to Ramon's neck in pure, delighted relief and contentment, I would have laughed in the person's face, then sent them to an asylum. But so much had happened in the past few months. I had found out Theron and Ramon were my half-brothers, and I had become good friends with them.

I had mourned Ramon when I thought he had died.

Theron finally pulled back and looked him up and down. "But ... how?"

I stepped back too. "We saw you die," I repeated, still not believing he was right in front of us.

Ramon shook his head. "No, you saw me being engulfed by the fire and assumed I was dead. Hell, I would have assumed it too."

A couple of tears escaped. "You mean ... we left you there."

Ramon clasped a hand on my shoulder. "For all you knew, I was dead. I felt dead."

"How did you make it out?" Theron asked.

"When I crawled out of the fire, you guys were long gone, and most of my body was severely burned." He paused, a frown between his brows. "I don't think I would have lived if it weren't for Violet."

"Violet?" I asked, confused.

Ramon extended his hand to someone to the side.

A beautiful young woman with long, light brown hair and a cotton blouse and leather skirt covering her toned body walked toward him. Her hazel eyes fixed on his, she slipped her hand into Ramon's and he pulled her close.

"This is Violet," he said, with a small smile. "My mate."

I gasped.

Theron coughed. "Your ..."

"Mate," Ramon said again, confidence coloring the word. "You know, werewolves have mates."

"As in soulmates?" I asked, staring openly at the young woman. She wasn't much older than I was, and I had to admit, they look great together, but ... mate?

"Yes. Something like that." Ramon shifted his gaze to Violet. "She found me, and for some reason, she saved my life."

"For some reason." She scoffed, her eyes on his. She lifted her free hand and pointed at her chest. "I felt it in here. I *had* to save you."

The blistering love shining from their faces was too much. I took a large step back before I was burned.

Although it was all shocking and their love was too sugary, I was happy for Ramon. I was truly happy he had lived and found love and—

"Wait ... That was two months ago," I said. "You said you were badly injured." I looked around. I had no idea how many werewolves were in this pack, but by the looks of it, it was way more than a hundred. "How come you're the alpha?"

"Good question." Theron punched Ramon's shoulder. "You? Alpha?"

Theron went to punch Ramon again, but he twisted, smiling. "Well ..."

"The previous alpha didn't take it well when I brought Ramon to the pack," Violet said.

"She was promised to him," Ramon explained.

"Promised? As in the alpha's mate?" I asked.

Violet shook his head. "I wasn't his mate, but he had asked my father for my hand anyway. Because my father didn't want to refuse the alpha, he accepted." She glanced to Ramon again. "But when I found Ramon and helped him, I knew there was something more. And once he was in better shape and—"

Ramon cleared his throat. "Let's just say, we quickly found out she was my mate."

"Did you tell the previous alpha?" Theron asked.

Violet shook her head. "He was a mean, cold hearted werewolf. Most of us were afraid of him. We didn't defy him unless it was necessary." She paused. "And his mood only soured when I brought a stranger into the pack. Later when he found out Ramon had been a tzigane who was transformed into a werewolf through alchemy, he was livid. He wanted to kill Ramon on the spot."

"She intervened," Ramon continued. "She promised him she would marry him right away if he let me leave instead. So, he ordered me to go."

All right, this sounded like a romantic story, and despite it being about my brother, I was into it. "What did you do?"

"I didn't have a choice," Ramon said. "Because of the alpha's command, the entire pack had to turn against me and I was pushed away."

Theron frowned. "When was that?"

"Two weeks ago," Ramon said.

I gestured toward him. "And how did you get here?"

"I didn't want to leave Violet. I couldn't bear to imagine her with the previous alpha. On top of that, during my short time in the pack, I had learned he was a terrible leader. The werewolves only did his bidding because they were afraid of him." The corner of his lips tugged up. "So, I got ready and came back to challenge him."

"I see you won." Theron punched Ramon's upper arm. What was with men and punching? "Well done, punk."

"It wasn't easy," Ramon said. "But I was able to defeat him."

Violet rolled her eyes. "The battle lasted ten hours. By the end, both of them were exhausted."

"Ten hours?" I cried.

"So you've been alpha for how long?" Theron asked? "A week?"

"Five days," Ramon said, feeling proud of himself.

"He's new to the position, but we can tell the other werewolves are more at ease with him as our leader," Violet said, pride stamping her voice. "They already look up to him."

I shook my head, trying to wrap my mind around all of this. I was still trying to catch up with the whole Ramon-is-alive thing, but the fact that he had lived his own adventure the past two months ... which brought a halting thought.

I punched Ramon on the arm, just like Theron had done before. "Why did you let us think you were dead for so long?" I punched him again. "We mourned you. You had rituals done for you. We cried for you."

Ramon's shoulders sagged. "I'm really sorry I didn't send word. It took me a long time to recover, and by the time I was well enough to walk on my own, I was already in trouble with the previous alpha. I wanted to send a message, but the only way was to leave, and I couldn't do that." He briefly glanced at Violet. "And when I was kicked out, I knew I didn't have much time to come back and fix things. But a couple of days ago, I sent a message to the enclave, but my werewolves came back saying you and some of our friends were missing." He glanced to the rest of our group. "So, I sent my werewolves to find you."

"Why attack us?" Artan asked, crossing his arms. "They could have just told us they were bringing us to you."

Ramon shrugged. "What was the fun in that?" I punched his shoulder again. "Ouch. Mi, stop." He looked out at the others again. "You aren't hurt, are you?" Everyone quickly muttered "no" and shook their heads. "Then tell me, what happened? Why are you running from the enclave?"

My stomach hurt with hunger and I pressed a hand over it. "Can we please talk while we eat? Tell me you have food to spare?"

Ramon chuckled. "Of course. When I knew you were being brought here, I had a feast prepared for you." He gestured for us to follow him. "Let's eat."

14

———————

I MOVED IN BED AGAINST KANE'S BODY, AND FOR A MOMENT, almost forgot where we were and what had happened. I turned to him, still sleeping, and stared at his peaceful, handsome face. Like this, I could pretend everything was all right.

But it wasn't.

Last night, I told Ramon everything that had happened over the past two months he had been gone, including the fire heart fever, which actually had started before we had believed he died. We all agreed that we had to take down the council, but we didn't know how. We didn't want more hurt and death, so that was off the table, but we had to find a way to strip them of their authority and punish them. Hopefully, they would learn their lesson and leave us alone.

But it wasn't an easy thing.

For centuries, the enclaves had looked up to their elder councils; respecting the wiser elders was ingrained in tzigane Romani culture. If we tried to take down the council of our enclave, the rest of the tziganes might side with them and cause us trouble. And we couldn't go against the entire enclave.

Without an answer, we were taken to the guest quarters, where Ramon and Violet showed us to our bedrooms—large spaces carved out in the rocks with mattresses and blankets and a flimsy leather flap for door.

Despite the lack of security and the feel of having no privacy whatsoever, I had slept in Kane's arms and dreamed of a better, more just life.

And quieter too.

"What are you looking at?" Kane whispered, his eyes still closed.

"How do you know I'm looking at you?"

"I can feel the weight of your gaze."

I frowned. "Is it bad? A bad weight?"

He wrapped his arm around my back and pulled me even closer to him. "Not at all." He buried his face in my neck, grazing his nose on my skin, and ripping a shiver from me. "How about we stay in bed all day?"

I really liked that idea.

In fact, I liked the idea of being here and ignoring my duties way too much.

That was why I pushed away from Kane and stood up. "Unfortunately, we have too much to do."

"You're right," Kane said, his voice tight. Had I hurt his feelings? That hadn't been my intention. He shot up from the mattress and changed.

I found some clothes Violet had brought over last night and looked them over. Most seemed flimsy and girly. At least, there was some leather pants and tunics among them. That would do.

I put the tunic over my head, suddenly remembering how tense Kane was last night, surrounded by dozens of werewolves. As a master slayer, he probably felt an urge to kill them all on sight. We had talked about it before bed, but he hadn't said much then.

"How are you feeling? I mean, about being in a den full of werewolves?"

His hands froze on the zipper of his pants. "Still tense and a little worried, but I trusted Ramon before—" He pressed his lips tight. Before his death, that was what he was going to say. "So I'm trying to give him the benefit of the doubt now and trust him again." He flexed his hands twice, three times. "But it's hard. My instincts are fighting me every two seconds."

I pulled down my tunic and offered him a soft smile. "I'm sorry this is so hard. Hopefully, you'll get used to it fast."

"Hopefully," Kane muttered.

I had finished zipping up my pants when Kizzy poked her head past the flap used as door.

"Are you awake?" Her voice already carried a happy singsong tone to it this early in the morning.

I felt like spewing a string of curses upon her, but thankfully, Kane noticed my distress and acted faster. "Yes, we're up." He was also dressed and reaching for his swords. Dang, if he had been naked, or even shirtless, I would have ... I didn't know what I would have done. Kizzy was too sweet and clueless and didn't deserve the spike in my temper. "What's up?"

"Violet told us breakfast will be served in the main cavern in thirty minutes, and later, she'll take the females for a stroll in the market. According to her, it's the most fun place in the den." She sounded excited.

Meanwhile, my mind got hung up on a couple of words.

Females? Market? Fun place? I appreciated Ramon taking us in, but I wasn't sure we should stay long either. This place was strange to us, with odd customs and rules, and the longer we stayed in one place, the more chance we gave Damara to catch up with us.

Kizzy's face fell serious.

"What?" I asked, worried. If she had lost her smile and her sparkle, then things were bad. "What happened?"

"You're going to wear that?" She pointed to me.

I looked down at my pants and tunic and boots. "Hm, yeah."

"Didn't you receive the clothes from Violet last night? There were dresses in my bag." She twirled around, and the skirt of her pink dress rose in the air, almost like a ballerina's tutu. "Isn't it pretty?"

It was, but it wasn't practical. We were at war, or at least preparing for one. I felt more comfortable in clothes I could fight in. "Very."

She marched into the room. "Then let's get you changed." All business, she advanced on me.

"No, but ... Kane ..."

"Kane will agree with me," Kizzy said, looking for the bag with the colorful dresses. "A makeover is everything a girl needs to feel powerful and confident again."

"No, wait—"

He waved me off. "I'll wait for you in the main cavern."

The traitor exited our room, leaving me alone with the monster who was about to wreak havoc on my schedule.

I tried reasoning with her. "You know I have to talk to Ramon and the others about our next steps, right?"

"I know." Kizzy nodded as she picked up the bag from the

floor and started rummaging through it. "And I also know that Ramon is busy with some hearings, and Violet wants to spend some time with us." She pulled out a dark red dress with burnt orange details and held it in front of me. "This color will look great with your complexion and hair."

Gently, I pushed the dress down. "Kizzy, I too have things to do. The land is dying and the elder council is trying to kill me, not to mention Damara and her army are hunting for me as we speak. I can't sit down and play makeover."

For the first time since knowing her, Kizzy put her hands on her waist and gave me a hard look. "I understand what's going on, Mi, and I understand the weight of *everything* rests on your shoulders. But you're only one tzigane. If you don't stop to take care of your body and soul, you'll crumble. And if you go down, all of us go down. Taking a day off to recharge, while *thinking* about strategies might do you more good than you think."

I stared at her, wondering what was going on. Where was the bubbly Kizzy, and where did this wise girl standing in front of me come from? Despite knowing her words carried truth, I couldn't push aside my responsibilities like that. "I understand, but—"

She pushed me down to a chair. "No buts. Just enjoy this."

I was about to protest more when the flap serving as a door moved and Ellie stepped inside. She lifted an eyebrow. "What's going on?"

"I'm giving Mirella a makeover," Kizzy said, the enthusiastic note back to her voice.

"Oh, that's fun." Ellie walked toward us. "Can I help?"

Kizzy smiled. "Sure!"

"No!" I snapped.

Ellie chuckled. "This will be fun."

I met Ellie's eyes through the mirror, giving her the best pained stare I could conjure, but my best friend shrugged. Apparently, she was having way too much fun with this.

"You're dead," I mouthed, which only made Ellie chuckle again.

———

TWENTY-FIVE MINUTES LATER, I LOOKED AT MYSELF IN THE mirror and I had to admit, maybe Kizzy had a point. Since the festival, I hadn't had a decent shower, or brushed my hair with care. Clothes? I put on anything I could find.

The Mirella staring back at me looked more like the dancer Mirella of seven months ago, ready to go on stage or even a catwalk.

Kizzy had brushed my hair vigorously, making it look luscious and voluminous in a way I hadn't seen in a while. She had pulled the top half of my hair back and added braids to it, entwining them all in one thick braid that fell over the rest down my back.

Then, she cleaned my face and applied some light makeup. I begged her to not go crazy there and thankfully she listened to me. I could see some highlights on my cheeks, a little gold shadow on my eyelids, and the soft pink lipstick, but I still looked like myself.

Like most tzigane, I also sported big golden hoops on my ears, and several bracelets on my arms. Then there was the dress. It was a pretty thing with a tight bodice with loose, short sleeves, and flowy skirt. It fell down to the middle of my shins, which Kizzy was happy about, so could show off the golden sandals she had found for me.

The result was good, great even, but ... "Isn't this too much for breakfast?"

"Nonsense." Kizzy clasped a long leaf-like earring to her ear. She and Ellie had also dressed up and applied some makeup. "We'll look great for our day off."

Would the others take a day off too? I would feel bad if they didn't. Cora and Trina had stopped by, looking for us, but once Kizzy mentioned the makeover, Cora had bolted and Trina had excused herself, saying she could dress up and do her own makeup.

A knot fell between my brows. "Where did you get all of this?" I finally asked. There wasn't any makeup or jewelry in the bag Violet had handed us last night.

The corners of Kizzy's lips slid into a naughty smile. "I woke up early this morning and asked Violet for supplies. She has so many things! You guys should see it. They have a closet full of everything. It's like they are waiting for ... what's that human holiday where they dress up and go asking for candy? Hallows Eve?"

"Halloween," Ellie said. "My favorite holiday."

"Mine too," I whispered.

Kizzy gasped. "By Saint Sara-la-Kali, we'll be late for breakfast. Let's go."

We rushed to the main cavern, where all our friends were gathered. They had been engrossed in conversation, but the moment the three of us stepped into the room, they stopped and ogled us.

"Well, may I ask what the special occasion is?" Ramon asked, clearly amused by our outfits.

I knew it. I knew we shouldn't have dressed up this much to spend the day locked inside a werewolf den.

But when I locked eyes with Kane, who was seated at the

table, his shoulders squared and his arms tense, I realized this wasn't so bad. He stared at me with pure heat in his hazel eyes. Warmth spread over me, and I had the urge to invite him back to our room.

But then Violet strolled into the cavern, wearing a long purple dress, her hair in a beautiful brown cascade over her shoulders, and bright red staining her full lips. If I had found her beautiful before, now I believed she was stunning.

"I asked the girls to dress up," she said.

Ramon's jaw dropped. "W-why?"

Violet stopped at our side. "Nothing special. We're just going to the market and have a fun day planned." She linked arms with Kizzy and me. "Come on, girls." She steered us away. "Cora, Trina, you're welcome to join us."

I thought Cora and Trina would scoff at us, but to my surprise, they got up and join us.

Violet guided us down a series of paths and short tunnels, until we arrived at a long, but narrow room busting with life and colors. In a way, this place reminded me of the stands at the spring festival, with its many tables of food, drinks, perfumes, jewelry, painting, leatherwork, and much more. People milled about, chatting and selling and buying and laughing. Kids ran and played. The only difference was that here the market was enclosed by walls and a ceiling made of rock.

Even Felix was here, lazing around between two stands, some kids playing around him and climbing over him. And he seemed happy about that.

I chuckled. It was only yesterday that he was tense entering a werewolf den, now he was here, playing with them as if this were a regular occurrence.

I looked around. They really looking like regular humans.

Well, they *were* regular humans. Like us, the tziganes—we all had something that made us special, but we were still the same on the inside.

Violet took us from stand to stand, introducing us to her people, giving us bits of food and drink to try, and applying perfume to our hair, and hanging shawls over our necks and telling us we looked beautiful. It was fun and carefree and mildly entertaining.

But I couldn't help noticing the two warriors in our midst. Cora might not have dressed up, but she at least mixed well with us, touching the items, tasting the food, and commenting when she liked or didn't like something.

Trina barely spoke. Her steps were hard, as if it hurt her to walk with us. I could see how tense she was in the hard set of her shoulders.

Something was bothering her, and I was dying to ask her what it was.

But before I could summon the courage to say anything, I halted in front of a stand with flowers—daisies, poppies, orchids, roses—and right behind the stand was a tall painting of the heart flower.

An old woman smiled at me. "Unusual, isn't it?" I nodded. "It's called the heart flower and it's supposed to be magical." She narrowed her eyes at me. "Aren't you a tzigane?"

"Y-yes," I mumbled. Of course, most of werewolves had seen us arriving yesterday. They all probably knew who we were and why we were here.

"Then you know all about this flower."

"I sure do." More than she would ever imagine. "Does this flower have a special meaning to werewolves?"

She shook her head. "No, not really. It's just a very pretty and unusual flower. I have been alive for many, many years and never saw one with my own eyes."

A young woman stepped to my side and asked the old woman for a bouquet of flowers. "Excuse me," she said, turning to her client.

I stared at the painting for a moment longer, still shocked the heart flower would get the attention of werewolves, then forced my steps forward.

The girls were already a few stands ahead of me.

I started walking faster to catch up, but then Trina fell into step with me, her shoulders tight.

"What is it?" I asked, though it wasn't the question burning my tongue.

Her answer surprised me. "Mirella, I know you followed me the other night." I skidded to a halt; my eyes bugged. Trina pressed her lips tight, before continuing, "I know you saw me at the lake, and you know I talked to someone using alchemy."

"All right, I won't lie," I said. "It was me. Will you tell me what you were doing?"

She shook her head. "I can't. Please, Mirella, I beg you, just trust me. And no matter what happens next, don't follow me again. It's too dangerous."

"What do you mean?"

"I can't tell you," she whispered as if saying just that was already too much, as if it hurt her. "Please, just do what I say. Don't follow me again." She took a step back. "I'm sorry."

With a pained glance, Trina spun around and disappeared between the market stands. I stayed rooted to the ground for a moment, in shock. How could she ask me that? Not just about following her, but to trust her without any real explanation. I wanted to trust her; I really did.

But something in my chest tightened and I found I couldn't.

Trina was hiding something and I knew it wasn't a small thing.

15

THE NEXT MORNING, I GOT UP EARLY AND GOT DRESSED IN regular leather pants, a shirt, and thick boots. I tied my hair into tight braid and made sure I had no jewelry on. I had to admit that yesterday had been a fun, different day, something my soul needed to recharge, but if Kizzy came in pushing for another makeover and day off, I would send her to hell.

The time for rest was over.

We had to get ready for war.

Before breakfast, I met with Ramon alone in the living room of his home—a series of rooms and tunnels carved out on the rocks inside the mountain. It was an odd place, and if I stopped to think about it, I became claustrophobic, but he and Violet had added a lot of comfort and details to the walls and floors, and it almost looked like a regular house.

Ramon and I discussed the challenges ahead of us and how to solve them.

"Let's hope it works," Ramon said, getting up from the couch. Violet stepped into the room and approached us.

Ramon smiled at her and placed his hand on her belly. "For all of our sakes, I hope it works."

I gasped. "By Saint Sara-la-Kali. You're pregnant."

It wasn't a question, but Violet nodded, smiling. "We found out a couple of nights ago."

I embraced the two of them tight. "Congratulations. That's amazing." I pulled back and narrowed my eyes at my brother. "It is amazing, right?"

He chuckled. "It is. Really amazing. But it also makes me more cautious and eager to finish this soon."

I nodded. "I understand." I looked at Violet then Ramon. "Don't worry. You don't have to get more involved than what we talked about. And if things go south, you just grab your family and run."

Ramon didn't like fleeing from a fight, but I thought that for the first time, he wouldn't be against it.

Later, the three of us marched into the main cavern and found our friends seated at a table, waiting for us.

Upon seeing me, Kizzy pouted. "I thought you learned something and would wear more dresses."

I held back a smile. "I can't fight in a dress and we're getting ready for a big fight now." Under my friends' gaze, I took my place beside Kane. He immediately reached for me, holding my hand in his. "Eat," I told them. "I would rather wait until they were full to talk, in case someone lost their appetite. I needed strong warriors beside me. "We'll talk soon."

A big breakfast was laid on the table in front of us, complete with eggs, bacon, and bagels. There was also a variety of things for the werewolves, but what really got my attention was the meat. Large pieces of steak ranging from raw to medium rare. Which was odd, because when Ramon lived with us, he didn't crave raw meat like this—unless he had contained his hunger for our sake—but right now, he devoured a blood dripping piece of meat.

My stomach churned, and I pushed my eggs back, not sure I could eat anymore.

I watched the people seated around the table. In this setting, having a good meal, my friends almost looked relaxed, happy. Ramon held Violet's hand across the table, Kizzy smiled at Artan, Rye pampered Cora while she pretended she didn't care, Theron laughed over some nonsense Ellie said, Kane sat by my side, unflinching and ready for anything I threw his way. Even Felix, who had been as tense as Kane when we first joined the werewolves, looked relaxed as he lounged beside the table, devouring his own piece of raw meat.

Trina was the only one who was serious and kept glancing at me, as if she expected me to shoot up and tell everyone she had sneaked out of the cabin a few nights ago.

I frowned. I was sure that wasn't the way to gain her trust, though, at the moment, I wasn't sure of anything. How could I show her she could confide in me? That whatever it was, I would help her with it? That she didn't need to do it alone?

I waited a little longer, until most of them looked like they were done, to start the meeting.

Ramon cleared his throat, calling everyone's attention. A somber silence fell over the room. "Mirella and I have a lot to discuss with you all."

Like a cloak of seriousness had fallen over us, everyone straightened in their chairs and pushed their plates away. They looked at Ramon and me, ready for whatever battle may lay ahead.

My heart swelled with pride. "There are a couple of

things we need to solve. We need to decide what to do about the elder council, we need to get ready for a war with Damara, and we need to reverse the ceremony and stop the land from dying." The last item was all on me, but I wouldn't mind if my friends helped me.

"Don't forget about you," Kane said. "We need to find a remedy for the fire heart fever."

"I'm not too worried about that right now." I winked at him. "Just stay close and I should remain sane until all of this is done. Then, when we fix everything, I'll worry about the fire heart fever."

"I agree there's no urgency to work on that," Theron said. "But we definitely can't forget about it."

Ellie nodded. "Yes, that will be our top priority after we deal with the rest."

Everyone murmured their agreements.

Warmth spread through my chest. I was glad to see my friends cared about me.

I took a long breath and continued, "Although we can't delay dealing with the elder council and Damara, I think reversing the spell on the land is the most important right now since everything is dying. If we end up confronting the council or Damara, we might take longer than expected, and the darkness will only spread further."

Again, everyone agreed with the plan so far.

"Okay, and how will you reverse the ceremony?" Artan asked, a cold edge to his voice.

That was the hard part. "I think I need to redo the ceremony, and for that, I need a heart flower."

Silence fell over us. Everyone looked at each other, knowing the main problem we had with this, but not voicing it.

Until Ellie broke the silence. "I'm guessing you haven't sensed a new heart flower."

I shook my head. "No."

"Was there a flower left at the enclave?" Theron asked.

"No," I said. "I mean, I'm not one hundred percent sure, but Darcy was supposed to have them all out for the ceremony."

"Even if there was one heart flower there, how would we sneak inside and steal a heart flower from right under their noses?" Trina asked.

I looked at her, my stance guarded. Since the day before, I had been even more suspicious. What was she doing and why did she ask me not to follow? How bad was it that she had gone out of her way to give me that warning? Or ... could it be that she wanted me to do the exact opposite? Right now, I wasn't sure of anything when it came to her, and I hated the foreboding feeling that something wasn't right.

"We have allies," Cora said. "Sheila, Dolan, Marisa, Leander, Lash, to name a few."

"But how do we get word to them?" Rye asked. "We ditched our phones a while back."

Phones were a rare commodity in the enclaves. Most tziganes never had them. In my case, I used it less and less. I hadn't touched mine since before the festival. If I had to guess, it was sitting on the nightstand inside my cabin on the edge of the enclave. The few of us who had brought phones had left them either at Ellie's mountain cabin, or lost them when we had been attacked by the werewolves.

Artan looked at Ramon. "Do you have a cell phone down here?"

Ramon shook his head. "There's no reason to. Phones

don't work down here, and when we're out, the chances are we'll shift and we won't be able to carry a phone anyway."

"Good point," Cora mumbled.

Theron groaned. "Here." He placed an outdated flip phone on the table.

"Where did you get that?" Kane asked.

"My father gave it to me before we left the enclave," Theron said. "He knew we might need to communicate in case of an emergency, but he didn't want to risk having us using our modern, traceable phones, so he bought two of these burner phones. One for me, one for him." He opened the phone and stared at its tiny screen. "I've sent him a couple of messages to let him know we're okay." He pushed the phone toward me. "But I guess this qualifies as an emergency and we should actually call him."

"Call him right now," Artan said. "Ask him to find out if there's still a heart flower there."

"And if there is, how do you suggest he grab it and get away with it?" Trina asked, once more referencing to leaving the enclave. "Do you think the elders or warriors won't be watching him?"

"I think that we should take this step by step," Kane said. "First, we find out if the elder council is holding another heart flower. If they are, then we figure out how to get the flower."

"I like that idea." I picked up the phone, as if I was holding a precious jewel. "I should go outside to make a call, right?"

Ramon nodded. "Yes. To be honest, you won't find any reception around here. You might have to walk a few miles toward the nearest road or town."

Shit. I exhaled. "It's fine. It'll be worth it." With the phone in my hand, I stood. "I should get going then."

Kane unfolded beside me. "I'm going with you."

I shook my head. "You're still hurt from—" I pressed my mouth shut. I didn't want to keep saying the T word. It brought forth too many bad memories, for the both of us. "You should rest."

"You might need to go too far from me," Kane said. "It's better if I'm with you."

"He's right, Mi," Ramon said. "At the base of the mountain, we have a car hidden, for emergencies. You can take it, if it still works, and drive to the nearest town instead of walking all the way there. That should save you some time."

"Sounds good." I glanced at Kane, still not liking that he would have to hike down the mountain with me. "Let's go."

16

IT TOOK A FEW TRIES FOR THE CAR, WHICH HAD BEEN EXPERTLY hidden behind tall bushes and covered in vines, to start. Kane was ready to throw in the towel, when finally, the engine sputtered to life and the entire car trembled.

Thank Saint Sara-la-Kali.

We had hiked down the mountain, with a heavy can of gas, for over an hour before finding the car, and despite putting on a brave face and hiding his pain, I could see how Kane braced himself with each step. After a while, his breathing grew labored and sweat beaded on his forehead. I wanted to stop and rest, but I knew that if I mentioned something like that, it would only hurt him more. So, I pretended I didn't see anything. Although, in my mind, I set a timer. If we didn't find the car by noon, I would break for a rest even if he threw a tantrum.

I glanced at Kane behind the wheel as he smiled at me, glad that the car was working. I couldn't see him having a tantrum, not even as a child. In my mind, he had always been stoic and brave and wise.

"Let's give this a try," he said, putting the stick shift into first. The car trembled again, but it moved forward.

I sighed in relief and checked the flip phone one more time.

Since we had left the werewolf den, I kept glancing at the phone, waiting for the bars to come up, but they never did. Even now, in the car, there was no signal. Which meant we had to keep going.

"There should be a road a couple of miles from here," I told Kane, pointing southeast. That was the direction in which Ramon had showed us the road and the next town on a map. "Hopefully, we'll have a signal before we reach the road."

"Hopefully," Kane repeated my prayer. Focused on the uneven ground ahead of us, he steered the car through the trees and over low bushes and branches. It would be a miracle if the car lasted longer than two minutes like this.

It was a miracle. The car held on as the terrain grew more even, and the trees became sparser. And the phone continued without bars.

I frowned. "I'm starting to wonder if this phone stills works."

Kane glanced at me for a quick second. "Isn't it new?"

"It is, I mean, the phone per se. Not the model." I let out a chuckle over my stupid joke. Because really who still sold flip phones?

Kane rolled his eyes at me. "Just keep checking the damn thing."

I would, but since we had nothing else to do other than sit here and drive to the road, I stared at him instead. I liked how he looked in the driver's seat, holding on to the wheel, the muscles of his arms popping every couple of seconds, his hazel eyes staring straight ahead. This was the first time I saw Kane wearing a short sleeve T-shirt, but even that looked fine on him. By Saint Sara-la-Kali, I suddenly wished I had the opportunity of seeing him wearing a suit—though tziganes never wore suits. I just knew Kane would look damn fine in one.

A beep came from the phone. I froze for a second before flipping it open and checking it. Half of the bars were up and there was a new text message.

I opened the text from the only phone number saved on the phone, named D.

Things continue the same here. The council still thinks we helped you leave and are hovering over us every second, night and day.

How are you?

D. Dolan or *dat,* for father.

It was a text from my father.

"You can stop the car," I told Kane, my eyes on the phone.

"Just because I can see the road ahead," Kane joked, but he brought the car to a stop.

I glanced up, and true enough, the road cut through the forest a few yards ahead. It was better this way. If we stayed just off the road, there was less of a chance humans would see us. The last thing I wanted was to involve humans in this mess.

"There's a text from Dolan." I showed Kane the phone and he read the message. "He said the council has been watching them all closely. They are suspicious."

"As we thought they would."

"But that means it'll be hard for them to check if there is a heart flower there. Much less steal one."

Twisting his body so he was facing me, Kane reached over

and placed his hand on my leg. "I bet your parents and almost any tzigane would do anything for you, and I'm pretty sure that if you ask something, they know it's because it's important."

Finding a heart flower was imperative. Kane was right. Everyone had to do their part in this war, and I needed to be able to let them. That meant, being okay with my parents doing more than watching me and supporting me from the sidelines.

I didn't like it, but it was necessary. "Should I reply, or call?"

"Call," Kane said. "It's better to explain everything to him talking than through text."

Holding my breath, I pressed the call button. The phone rang twice and then Dolan's voice came from the other side. "Theron? What happened?"

"It's me," I said, my voice trembling.

"Mirella? Are you okay? Where's Theron?" his words were shushed, and I wondered if he was being watched, or if he was being cautions.

"Dad ..." I didn't call him father or dad often, but for some reason, it felt right. "I need a favor."

I FLIPPED THE PHONE AND CHECKED IT AGAIN.

"That's the tenth time in less than two minutes." Kane snatched the phone from me. "He'll call when he can."

"But what if he was caught? What if Darcy is now torturing him?"

Kane cupped my face, making me stare into his eyes. "Trust him. Trust that they can do this."

It wasn't easy. I had sent my parents or whoever else they had asked to help to check if the elder council was still holding on to a heart flower. Which meant, they had to sneak into the administrative building and find the flower—or no flower—while the council and the warriors watched their every move. How would they do it? I had sent them into a trap.

Because the phone wouldn't work if we returned to the den, Kane and I agreed to stay here for a couple of hours. My father had two hours to call us and let us know if they had found a flower or not. If he didn't call back in two hours—

I stopped my thoughts there. I couldn't think like that or I would drive myself sick with worry.

Like Kane said, I had to believe in them. To trust them. They might not be super young anymore, but they were strong and resourceful.

They could do it.

"You're right," I muttered. "As usual."

One corner of his lips tugged up and he lowered his hands. "As usual. I like that. I could get used to that."

I slapped his shoulder, rather soft, but Kane groaned. I pressed my hand to my mouth. "I'm sorry. Shit, I'm sorry."

"It's okay." Kane rolled his shoulder and groaned again. "It'll be okay, eventually, I hope."

A feeling bloomed in my chest and a new thought snaked its way in my mind. Back a few months ago when Cora had had some crazy nightmare about her family and her enclave, I had helped her calm down using my magic. I couldn't heal anyone, but I could sooth them if I controlled my fire the right way. But Kane was different. We hadn't tested it with a direct hit, but each time Kane and I had slept together, my fire had burned through my skin and it had never hurt him.

I wondered …

I folded my legs under me in the passenger seat, and scooted closer to him. "I want to try something." One of Kane's eyebrows shot up. I chuckled. "It's not what you're thinking!" Careful not to hurt him, I grabbed his shoulders and adjusted him in front of me. "Just relax." I pressed my palm to the center of his chest and called on my fire. "Tell me if it hurts."

I sent my fire into him. He closed his eyes as my fire spread, taking in every inch of his body. "Hm, no, it feels good."

With my mind set on healing and making him better, I kept my fire flowing into him. Feeding him. Warming him. Healing him. "Is it better?"

Kane lifted the hem of his shirt. The purple bruise spread over his stomach slowly faded away, until finally it disappeared, leaving behind only beautiful golden skin and hard muscles.

"It's … incredible." He rolled his shoulders. "No aches or pains anymore. I feel like new." He fixed his eyes on mine, a molten gleam shining from them. "You're incredible."

I withdrew my hand. "Nah, it's just magic. Although, I don't think this would have worked with anyone else."

"I don't think so either." He crossed over the console between the seats and crawled to me.

My eyes widened and I retreated, gluing my back to the door. "What are you doing?"

"Why?" He wrapped one arm around my waist and slid me down, so he was half over me. "Don't you want it?"

"I-I do," I confessed, my voice raspy, my heartbeat accelerating. That was what I got when he was so near me, holding me and staring at me like he was hungry. For me. "But in the car—"

"We've made love in several places already. Why not a car?" He lowered his head toward mine. I thought he would kiss me, but he halted, his lips just an inch from mine. "Doesn't this adventure make you feel more excited? More aroused?" A ripple of desire course through my body. "You don't want it? Just tell me and I'll back off."

I wound my arms around his neck and pulled him closer to me. "Don't you dare?"

Kane was smiling when his lips crushed over mine. The kiss began soft, slow, the rhythm intoxicating, exhilarating. But this wasn't us, not most of the time. My lips parted more and Kane's tongue invaded my mouth. He deepened the kiss, moving his lips hard and deep against mine.

With swift moves, Kane carried me to the backseat. He lowered his body over mine and I moaned. Why was it so satisfying to feel his body pressed against mine?

I reached for the hem of his shirt and tugged. Breaking the kiss, Kane helped me slip it over his head. Before I could get rid of the shirt by tossing it aside, Kane pulled my shirt off. I giggled as I set it down, his mouth already back on mine.

But my laughter was short lived as he pressed his hard-on against my pelvis.

By Saint Sara-la-Kali.

I thought this would be a quick and hard sex session, and I was all for it, but then Kane broke the kiss and pulled back, enough to look into my eyes. He ran a hand through my hair and a small smile took over his lips.

"I love you," he said, firm and sure.

My heart stopped for a moment, then kicked up and beat faster. My eyes misted. "I love you too." It was the truth. Kane had come into my life out of nowhere and been there for me when I was alone and lost, and now I couldn't imagine my life without him. Sometimes, when I thought that he might think I was only with him because of his power over the fire heart fever, I panicked. I needed him to know he meant more to me, but not once had I had the courage to tell him my real feelings for him. Until now. "I love you so much."

"I love you more," he whispered.

Then, his mouth was on mine again. Deftly, he removed the rest of my clothes and made sweet, sweet love to me.

17

———

"It's going to be okay," Kane whispered in my ear.

He stood behind me as we glanced out at the clearing, waiting.

Yesterday, after making love to Kane, we still had to wait until my father called us back. I had no idea how they had made it, but he told me he had found a heart flower and they had snatched it from the administrative building. For now, the elder council didn't have any idea the flower was gone, but they didn't want to risk holding on to it for long. We agreed on meeting early this morning at a halfway point between the werewolf den and the Lovell enclave. Kane and I had made it back to the den, rested for a couple of hours, then had left again—this time with our friends. Ramon wanted to join us, but he decided to stay back with Violet, in case he was needed there.

The sun hadn't risen yet, and there were still a couple of minutes to the appointed time, but I couldn't stop my heart from pounding against my chest in worry.

What if they were caught? What if they were hurt?

"I know," I said, more to myself than to anyone else, and still the words didn't make me feel any less worried.

Kane pressed a kiss on my temple. "Just a little longer."

My friends and I stood among the trees, watching the clearing. We weren't necessarily hiding, but we didn't want to be out in the open either.

On my left, Felix let out a low growl.

"What is it boy?" I asked. He sent an image of an animal into my mind. A white fox with shimmering fur like his, watching us from across the clearing, hidden behind some bushes. "There's another heart animal here," I told the group, my voice low so I wouldn't scare the fox.

Felix and I shared a special bond, but I didn't know why. Was it because he was a heart animal, or because it was him, not what he was? I had never met another heart animal before, so I couldn't confirm anything.

Until now.

Knowing I could scare the fox if I came on too strong, I sent a whiff of my senses toward him. The animal stilled, the walls around his mind up but pliable, as if he wanted me to push and go in. So I did. Careful, I entered his mind.

Only, it wasn't a he. It was a she, and her name was Vira.

Hi, Vira, I'm Mirella, the heart maiden.

The fox kept her mind clear as she peeked her head out from beyond the bush. She was even more beautiful than in my mind.

"Nobody move," Theron said, his voice low.

Head low, eyes on me, the fox took a step forward.

Come on. I put my hand on Felix's big head. *I'm his friend, see? I can be your friend too.*

The fox advanced another step. And another. And another.

I folded down, kneeling on the ground, and stretched my hand forward, inviting the fox to come to me.

A ruffling sound spread from the bushes and the fox froze. When my mother burst from the trees, running and panting, the fox took off.

I had one second to be sad about it, then my thoughts were all about my mother. "Mom," I called out, meeting her in the center of the clearing. I clutched her arms. "What happened?"

"I'm just—" She inhaled deeply, trying to catch her breath. "I ran from the edge of the forest here." She paused. "I don't want to be out longer than necessary."

"So they won't suspect anything." It wasn't a question, but she nodded anyway. "How did you get out?"

She shook her head. "No time to explain." She pulled the small duffel bag's strap from around her shoulders and passed it to me. "I was afraid of accidentally touching it, so I put it in here. I hope it's not too squashed."

"It's okay if it is." I took the bag from her. "Thank you."

She pressed a hand to my face. "Anything for you. Now I better go back."

She simply turned around and started marching away. What the hell? "Mom, wait—"

She halted and my words died on my tongue.

Holding their sharp swords by their sides, warriors stepped into the clearing. Lots of warriors. Many more warriors than Lovell ever had.

"Oh no." My mother took a step back and pushed me back with her. "The elder council must have known something was going on."

"Who are they?" I asked, noticing several faces I had never seen before.

My friends advanced, forming a long line beside us.

"They are from the visiting enclaves," Theron said.

The fox, hidden beside the warriors, whimpered. A warrior glanced at her, and without hesitation, caught her by her neck. "Another heart animal. How interesting." He threw her between us, and the poor thing let out a shrill cry.

I made for her, but Kane grasped my arm and I stopped. "Don't," he whispered, a glare fixed on the warriors. "The moment you step away from us, they will grab you."

Rage coursed through me.

A tall warrior pointed his sword at us, his eyes scanning our group. Finally, his gaze settled on Artan. "Artan, what a pleasure seeing you here."

"What do you want, Andrei?" Artan asked with a bark.

"I want the heart maiden and the heart flower," Andrei said. "Behave, and no one will get hurt." He tsked. "Although, I can't guarantee how you'll fare once your *puri daj* gets her hands on you."

"I'm not afraid of my *puri daj*," Artan snarled.

"You should be." He twirled his sword in his hand. "Get them!"

The warriors charged, and I raised both my hands, bringing up a wall of fire. It was tall enough that the warriors couldn't jump through it, but not so tall it touched the leaves in the tree tops, hanging over the clearing, lest I ruined more than the grass underneath it and started a wildfire.

"I don't want to hurt you!" I shouted so the warriors could hear me through the crackling of the fire.

"You'll have to do better than that, heart maiden," Andrei replied. "You can't burn the entire forest. We'll simply go around the flames."

Shit.

"Someone help the fox!" I hissed. Promptly, Ellie and Kizzy shot forward and gently scooped up the fox, bringing her back to our line. I called on more power, more fire, and pushed the warriors back. "We won't surrender."

"Then we'll have to fight," Andrei said, sounding excited. "And we'll have to kill your friends."

Kane growled beside me. "Get ready. We fight."

Theron's eyes widened. "But they are people we know. Some are our friends."

"*Were* your friends," Kane corrected him.

"This is ridiculous." I shook my head. "We have enough to worry about. I don't want to have to fight more tziganes. We should be in this together, not working against each other."

"I agree," Theron said. "But until we take down the council, we'll remain divided."

"First, we worry about fighting the warriors." Artan unsheathed his sword. "But try to avoid hurting them too much."

I looked at my raised hands. "No fighting. You guys run. I'll try to keep the wall up and spread the flames more. That should buy you some time."

My mother's face paled. "No!"

Cora's eyebrows shot up. "What about you?"

"I'll run when they are closer," I said. "I'll keep bringing up fire walls and create a maze so can't get to me."

"I don't like it," Kane said.

"Yeah, I think it's risky," Rye said.

I glanced at my friends. The only one utterly still and quiet was Trina. What? Was this her secret? Was she working with the elder council and the warriors, waiting for an opportunity to snatch the bag with the flower from me? Or a way to disarm me and hand me over?

"If you stay, then I'll stay too," Kane said, adamant. I opened my mouth to complain but he cut me off. "If you end up running the opposite direction from us, then you'll be in bigger trouble." Meaning, I could get too far from him and be hit by the fire heart fever symptoms.

"Fine," I muttered. "But the others, you guys should run. Now!"

I sent more fire into the wall, extending it a little more across the forest, making it harder for the warriors to find its end.

My friends glanced at each other. They turned to leave.

A heavy shadow fell over the clearing, a chill breeze blew past.

A figure appeared from the shadows.

"Heart maiden." Muma Padurii smiled at me, showing off her jagged teeth. "I have been waiting for you."

My magic faltered, and remembering her last words to me, I let it go.

The fire wall faded into orange smoke, crinkling into the shadows.

My friends tensed beside me. Kane pulled me halfway behind him. "What do you want?" he asked, his voice firm.

"I've come for heart maiden."

WAS DEATH REALLY MY DESTINY? BECAUSE IT SURE SEEMED SO. If I didn't die by the elder council's hands, Damara and her minions were still out there, not to mention the regular alchemists who also would do anything to have the heart maiden's blood for their potions.

And now Muma Padurii.

I should probably tell them to take a number or get in line. Either way, it didn't seem like I was doing anything in the future other than dying.

Following Kane's initiative, my friends formed a wall in front of me, keeping the forest protector away from me.

I spied over their shoulders, trying to see what the mad woman would do. Not that I wanted to look at her gray barklike skin, long dirty black hair, and her hairy legs, but I couldn't help it. If she disappeared, then I had to be ready to defend myself.

"I told you, little heart maiden, that I would come for you if you hurt my forest again," Muma Padurii said, her voice carrying over the wind in an eerie tone. "You probably know you hurt my forest more than once since my warning, but I let it slide." She pointed to the ground beside us, a long black line staining the grass. "But you've done it again." I swallowed hard. Was she going to blame me for— "Now let's talk about the land dying. I know that was your doing."

I knew she would bring that up. Shit.

I raised my hands above my hand, like a surrender sign and walked forward. "I did that, yes." My friends tried staying in front of me, but I pushed them aside and moved past, only stopping when I was a couple of feet from the forest protector. Her heavy scent of leaves and roots and musk filled my nostrils. "You can't take me yet. There's too much I need to fix first." I hoped the begging tone of my voice was hint enough. "I need to save a lot of people. After I'm done ... when I'm done, you can come for me."

Muma seemed utterly bored. "I don't care about your people. I don't care about your enclave, or the wolf pack, or the red alchemists. As long as everyone stays out of my forests, I don't care about anything else."

I frowned, wondering what deal I could make with her. "What if I can reverse the dying land?"

"What do you mean?"

"I want to reverse the spell that affected the land. I think I can stop it from advancing and even bring back the dead land." I lifted my chin. "I'm certain I can. Actually, I'm the only one who can."

She lifted an eyebrow, her dark eyes glinting. "How?"

"I need to redo a spell and restore the land." I patted the duffel bag slung across my shoulders. "I have all the ingredients I need for that."

Muma thought for a second, then shook her head. "I gave you months to do better, to be better, but you always hurt my forest. This time, you've gone too far, heart maiden."

I pressed my eyes closed, forcing myself to say the next word. For some reason, my pride didn't want me to utter it. "Pl—"

"It would be helpful if you cured the land before I took you." She narrowed her eyes, thinking.

I held my breath, waiting and praying for her consent, but before she could say anything, the other warriors were back. With swords held high, they advanced on us. They either hadn't seen Muma Padurii, or they weren't shocked by her appearance. The only thing on their minds was to capture me alive.

With a bothered groan, Muma waved her hands. Thick vines sprouted from the ground and twisted around the warriors' bodies.

"What the—?"A vine twisted around Andrei's mouth, shutting him up.

"Here's the deal," Muma started, as if we weren't surrounded by a forest of warriors blooming from the center of vines like flowers. "If you can save the land within three hours, I'll forgive your debt. If you can't, I'll kill you and your friends."

I stiffened. "Not my friends. They didn't do anything."

"They are here with you, aren't they? And they have been with you every time you hurt my forest."

"But they aren't—"

"It's okay, Mi," Theron said. "You can do it, and we'll all be fine."

Now that they were added to the equation, I felt less sure.

What if I messed it up again? I could deal if I was the only one punished, but my friends too? Even my mother? Ellie? Kane? I couldn't deal with that.

A long vine sprouted from the ground, curling around Kane's legs. He jerked against it, but the vine only wrapped around him tighter.

"Muma!" I cried, clasping the growing vine. I would burn it all away until he was free.

"Hurt my vines and I won't make any deal," Muma warned. I dropped my hands, my fire dying under my skin. "As insurance, I'll keep the one you love the most." The others seemed a little taken aback, especially Artan, but I had already known. In my heart, I knew Kane meant more to me than I cared to admit. "Go, save the land, then I'll let him go in one piece."

Kane stopped moving and looked at me, his eyes serious. "It's okay. You can do it. I'll be fine."

My certainty wavered some more. So much depended on this damn ceremony. I couldn't fail twice.

"Go, Mirella," my mother said. "The sooner you start, the sooner we'll be back."

I couldn't break Kane's stare. "It's okay," he said again, a much softer edge to his usual rough voice. "Go."

I ran.

My friends followed me as I weaved through the forest. I only slowed down when I arrived at the top of the small hill, where Ramon paced beside a crude fire and a black pot.

"What took you so long?" he asked, his tone sharp. But then he must have seen something in my face and his shoulders sagged. "What happened?"

Without a word, I went to the pot and fire and glanced to

the other side of the hill. The darkness advanced fast, and in a less than thirty minutes, it would be on top of us.

I had to be fast.

A few paces behind me, our friends caught up with us. They stopped beside Ramon, a few feet to the side, giving me plenty of space to work.

Theron quickly told Ramon what had happened and why we were late, but thankfully they didn't elaborate on it.

Kizzy knelt. "Let me know if you need help."

Ellie sat on the grass beside her. "Me too."

"Thanks," I muttered. "But I think I need to do this alone."

My friends remained in silence as I worked. With laser sharp focus, I put the pot over the fire, controlling it with my magic, so it wouldn't burn me—not that it could, but when the fire wasn't mine, it hurt nonetheless. Next, I pulled out the heart flower from the duffel bag. From all the running, it was bent and broken, and as expected, some parts were missing. It wouldn't make any difference—I hoped.

I cut up the flower into little pieces, but before placing them in the pot, I closed my eyes and got lost inside my mind.

What had gone wrong the first time? I had been distracted. I had looked at Kizzy and seen how happy she was after having asked me to perform her wedding ceremony, how happy she was because she was getting married to the man she loved, to the man who I had once loved. At that moment, I had felt hurt, jealous. Hurt because of her lack of consideration, hurt over all the things that had gone wrong between Artan and me, hurt because it had ended in an ugly way. Jealous because she couldn't be happier and I wanted to feel like that, jealous because they seemed happy together and I wanted to feel that same happiness, jealous because they were careless and free and could enjoy being together and I wanted to be able to love someone and stroll around with him, showing my man off.

Although I had let Artan go months ago, I couldn't erase the past and the feelings it stirred.

And that had been the problem.

I opened my eyes and looked at the sky—I would have stared at Kane if he were here. But I had someone now, someone I cared for more than anything, someone I loved the most. I had someone who made me laugh, who cared for me, who made me feel protected. Someone who wanted to be with me and wasn't afraid of what others would say, see, or think.

My heart squeezed.

I had to get this right; I had to save him. Otherwise ...

I didn't know. I just knew I couldn't imagine a world without Kane.

Inhaling deeply, I filled my mind with good things. Kane, my mother, my family and friends, finding out Ramon was alive, the land healthy and beautiful, the enclave happy and unified and strong, my madness gone.

But most of all, I thought of spring and the heart flower.

I imagined the world full of heart flowers. I could easily pick them up and make heart elixirs for all the tziganes and stock up for centuries. No one would ever suffer from the heart disease anymore, even if for some reason it took another two hundred years for a new heart maiden to show up.

I imagined a world without revenants, where the alchemists were powerless and didn't attack us, where humans and tziganes lived in peace together.

Holding on to those thoughts, I threw the pieces of the

heart flower in the pot. Like before, an explosion shook the pot and colorful smoke rose from the pot, filling the air with a rainbow cloud.

"It worked," my friends whispered.

I held my breath and stared at the pot. The first time, I had thought it had worked too and then that bit of black smoke sputtered from the cauldron, only for a few seconds, but it had been a sign that things had gone wrong.

I waited and waited, and the pot only spilled the rainbow-like smoke.

My friends grew agitated, but they didn't interrupt or call out to me.

A long time passed and nothing else happened.

Slowly, I scooted back. "I think ... I think it worked."

I shot to my feet and went to the edge of the hill. My friends flanked me. Together, we watched the darkness, waiting for any move, any direction, any changes.

It advanced toward us an inch.

My chest deflated and my stomach bottomed out.

No, no, it couldn't be. This time, I had been focused and ready. I hadn't made a mistake; I was sure of it.

Ramon pointed at the darkness. "Look!"

It had stopped. The darkness had stopped advancing.

I held my breath. What now? It would just stop? Whatever was dead would remain like that? No, there had to be another way. There had to be another ceremony, another spell I could do to make it retreat and bring back all the life that was lost.

I turned, going for the pot, but Theron clasped my arm and pulled me back.

I stared at the darkness as it moved. It backed away

another inch. My heart stopped for a moment. Then it retreated another inch. And another inch. And one other.

I exhaled in relief. "It worked."

19

WHEN WE MADE IT BACK TO MUMA, THE WARRIORS WERE nowhere to be found, my mother still held the hurt fox, and Kane stood beside her, free of the vines.

He saw me coming and rushed to me. I threw myself in his arms, happy to see him okay. "You did it," he whispered in my ear. His hold was tight and sure. "I knew you could."

He pressed his lips on mine, but our reprieve was short lived when Muma spoke up.

"A deal is a deal," she said, loud and clear. Almost bored. "You were able to save the land. Your debt is forgiven." She stared at me, those black eyes giving me chills. "But be warned. I won't tolerate you maiming my forest. Treat it right and I might become an ally."

My eyes widened, but before I could inquire what she meant, she was gone. Taken away by the shadows from the trees.

"Do I want to know how she got rid of the warriors?"

Kane shook his head. "Just know they are alive."

Well, if she hadn't killed them, then I was okay with it.

A low growl came from the fox. I knelt beside my mother. "How is she?"

"I don't know," my mother said. "I can't see any visible wounds, but I think she got hurt on the inside when the warrior threw her."

Calling on my magic, I hovered my hands over the fox's body, trying to get a feel for anything. I didn't think I could heal her like I had healed Kane before, but perhaps I could help her, sooth her, make it less painful.

I brushed my hand over her soft, white fur. When I touched her left side, she whimpered. Like I had done with her mind, I tried reaching inside her body, hoping that somehow her organs and muscles talked to me, told me what was wrong.

But they didn't need to talk. I could feel it. Mostly from the fox mind, I knew what was wrong. One of her ribs was broken and it was pressing against her heart and lung. The pain that coursed through her each time she breathed deeply was excruciating.

I'm going to try something, I told her in her mind.

The fox let out a low yelp. Since she didn't send me any negative images, I took that as a yes.

Keeping my heat low, I imagined my fire as a thin rope, like a whip. Guiding it with my hand, I sent it inside the fox. It wrapped around the rib, and without warning, I pulled it to its correct position.

The fox let out a cry. She trembled in my mother's arms, but a moment later, she took a deep breath and most of the pain was gone.

I thought about getting branches and tying them around her chest to keep the bone in place, but since it was the ribs, there was no way of doing it effectively. She just needed a good rest.

You can go now, I told her. *You should be fine.*

An image appeared in my mind. It was me standing a few feet from where we were and the fox entangled in my legs, like she was my pet. My friend.

Like Felix.

As if to make sure I understood what she meant, Felix appeared in the vision, imitating the fox.

You want to stay with me? Like Felix?

The fox let out a short bark. A yes.

I smiled. *I would love that.*

After caressing her head, I stood. "She needs rest."

Rye promptly scooped her up from my mother's arms. "I've got her."

"Thanks."

I glanced around, worried about leaving like this. Then a thought hit me. I turned to my mother. "The elder council knew about you meeting with us. What will happen to the others?" To Dolan, to Sheila? To our friends? If the elder council got their hands on them, I couldn't imagine what they would do.

My mother rested a hand on her neck. "I don't want to even think about that."

I frowned. "Are you saying—?"

"Your father knew it was a risk," she said. "He knew we could be found out. He was ready. Hopefully, he and the others got away or are hiding."

My chest seized. Hopefully. So much relied on hope.

Theron and Ramon crowded us. "He's a fighter," Theron said. "Even if he's caught, he won't go down easily."

"Yes, but he's smart too," Ramon added. "I bet he wasn't caught. Most likely, he joined the rest of our allies and fled."

Holding Kizzy's hand, Artan stepped into our circle. "We should move."

"He's right," Kane said, standing directly behind me. "The elder council knows we've been up to something. When the warriors are late to report back, they will know something is wrong."

Trina finally joined the group. "What's the next step?"

I glanced at her, still concerned about whatever she was hiding.

"We should hit the elder council next," Theron said. "They will be expecting us, but it'll be easier to take them down and recover the enclave than face Damara with her revenants and red alchemists right now."

Ramon nodded. "Then let's go. Let's get back to the den, get cleaned up, and get ready for another battle."

20

It was just past noon when we got back to the den. Felix and Vira decided to stay outside, since the fox didn't feel comfortable being around so many werewolves—but she was okay with a lion? Well, I guess since Felix was also a heart animal, she had nothing to fear from him. I tried explaining the werewolves were friendly, but I understood her fear and let them be.

Inside, a table in the main cavern waited for us, full of food and drink. Violet stood beside it, watching us eat as if we had starved for two weeks.

"What's the plan?" Trina asked, her voice low. The feeling that something wasn't right hit me again. This secret was bothering me so much. I didn't know how others didn't see her change in behavior and demeanor, but it was crystal clear. I had to pull her aside and talk to her again. She had to let me in. If she was in trouble, I could help.

"We all should rest now," Ramon said, before taking a big bite of a steak dripping with blood. "We'll leave in a couple of hours."

Theron wiped his mouth with the back of his hand. "You mean, we won't wait for daybreak?"

Ramon shook his head, but since his mouth was full, Kane spoke up. "They will be expecting us in the morning."

"True," Artan said. "We usually attack in the mornings."

"So if we go at night, they won't be expecting us," Theron finished.

"Exactly." Ramon dropped his empty plate on the table.

My stomach tensed in little knots. "So we're just barging in? Attacking the elder council?"

Everyone looked at each other, confused. Only Artan lowered his gaze.

"What do you mean?" Cora asked.

I shrugged. "Shouldn't we try talking to them first?"

Theron stared at me with large eyes as if my madness was spilling from my brain right in front of them. "Have you already forgotten what they did to you?"

"Of course not," I snapped. How could I? It had been barbaric and painfully brutal. They had treated me like a lab rat, much like I imagined the alchemists would, including the death sentence hanging over my head, but ... "If we're going to take them down and install a new council, we need to be better than they ever were. We can't charge in there and threaten them and attack them." My friends seemed to consider this. "I honestly don't think they will listen to us or care what we say, but we should try."

"I agree," Artan spoke up. "I can help with the talking too." He lifted his gaze to us. "As much as I believe my *dat* and my *puri daj* are in the wrong in this matter, I don't want to see them hurt."

I hadn't suggested talking first because of that, but it was a good point. "We have to consider that the elder council is comprised of mothers and fathers and grandparents of a lot of tziganes from the enclave. If we don't go about this in a rational and peaceful way, the rest of the enclave might not side with us."

Kane glanced down at me. "You're right. We need to be better than they are."

Ramon's brows curled down. "I'll be honest, I don't like it. Like you said, I don't think they will listen to us. They will attack us first."

"Then we need to be ready," I said. "Try the peaceful way first, but be ready to defend ourselves, if necessary."

"So we load up on our magic and weapons, but only use them if needed," Rye said. "Got it."

The rest of the group muttered their agreements.

"All right." Ramon rose from his chair. "Let's rest now. Meet us at the den's main entrance in three hours."

The group dispersed. With his arm around my shoulders, keeping me close, Kane guided me back to our room.

"I doubt I'll be able to sleep," I said, resting my head on his shoulder.

"Well, you should at least lie down and close your eyes. Rest."

I glanced at him. "Will you be my pillow?"

A half smile spread over his lips. "Forever."

Kane leaned over me and I reached up on my tiptoes to meet him halfway. His lips brushed mine and—

An image flashed in my mind.

Felix and Vira, running inside the den, afraid and hurt. Hurt?

What happened? I asked into their minds.

Another image appeared to me.

Just outside the den, Damara stood among her red alchemists and revenants.

My legs wobbled.

"Damara," I rasped, my throat dry. "Damara is here."

"What?" Kane was shocked for a brief second. Then he was all action. He slipped his hand in mine. "Come on."

In a couple of minutes, we were back in the main cavern, our friends filling into the room, having heard Kane's shouts.

"What happened?" Ellie asked. "Something happened, right?"

A faint boom echoed from the tunnels and shook the den.

Kizzy eyes rounded. "What was that?"

"Damara and her minions are here," I announced.

"W-what?" Ramon paled.

Violet sank down on a chair. "That can't be."

Ellie shrank into Theron, and Kizzy hugged herself.

"How do you know?" Artan asked.

I pointed to the entrance two seconds before Felix and Vira burst through it. "They showed me."

Come here, I told Felix. The big lion skidded to a stop at my feet, breathing hard. Red stained his white coat. *What happened?* He showed me as he and Vira were lazing around the den's entrance, just under the rocks and out of the sun, when a heavy dark cloud covered the sun and figures stepped from the shadows. They jumped up and growled at Damara and her minions, but a red alchemist threw a small shadow blade toward them. Felix moved, but he wasn't fast enough. The blade grazed his back. After that, they ran inside the den and called to me. I examined the scratch on his back. It wasn't as bad as the blood made it look. He would heal in no time. *You'll be fine.*

Ramon looked at me, his dark eyes focused. "I'm going to help my people."

"And we will meet Damara at the entrance. Right?" I glanced around to my friends. "Right?"

Another boom shook the den, louder this time.

"It seems she's closer," Kane said.

"Then we have no time to waste," Theron said, before spinning around and running out.

We followed him to the largest part of the den, the first room we arrived in when we were escorted in, dodging the werewolves, mostly women and children, who ran deeper into the caves, trying to hide.

Male werewolves joined my friends and me as we raced to the entrance.

But when we got to the throne area, we were too late. The room was filled with revenants and red alchemists, and standing like a queen at the tunnel's mouth was Damara.

She smiled at me.

"How did she know where we were?" Theron asked, his eyes straight ahead, his sword ready in his hand.

"Did she know about the den before?" Artan asked.

Ramon shook his head. "Not that I know of." He glanced at Theron and me. "I think our link still works when I'm in wolf form, but I'm not sure since we haven't tried after I turned into an alpha." He pulled off his shirt. "If you need me, try it." He ripped off the rest of his clothes and shapeshifted.

In his wolf form, he let out a long, loud howl. His wolves joined the odd song, then they lunged at our enemies, starting the battle.

My friends advanced too, except for Ellie, Kizzy, and

Violet, who stayed back, helping the women and children to escape to the back of the den.

And through all the fighting and the groans and cries and clank of metal, Damara smiled at me. I stared at her, not willing to back down. A slight dizziness came over me as she pushed her senses against mine. She wanted to get into my mind, but I wouldn't let her. Not this time.

Two revenants lunged for me, breaking our staring contest, and I stepped back, avoiding their sharp claws. They came at me again, and I threw my hands out, sending fire bolts at them both. The bolts exploded against their chests, opening a hole that spread over their bodies. Soon, their skin turned orange and they became ashes at my feet.

I glanced up. Even though that was the easiest way to kill them, there were too many revenants inside the den. If I were to do that too many times, I would be drained of my strength and stamina fast.

I had to debilitate them and hope Kane or Theron or whoever cut their heads out, effectively killing them.

Or …

A revenant snarled at me, before grasping for my neck. I ducked underneath its arm, spinning out of its range. To buy myself more time, I kicked its side hard. The revenant stumbled back, putting a couple more feet between us.

With no time to waste, I tested my new theory. I raised my hand and sent a small fire snaked toward the revenant. It slapped against the fire, but the snake was pure magic. It kept going until it wrapped around the revenant's neck. I clenched my fist and the snake constricted. The revenant shrieked as it clawed its neck, trying to get rid of the snake. But it couldn't. The fire snake tightened, melting into its skin. Like a fiery sword, the snake cut through the revenant's neck. Its head fell on the rocky ground, followed by his body.

I stepped back, my stomach revolving at the sight. At least, the spell had worked, and it didn't use much of my magic.

I turned, ready to enact the spell on two more revenants.

A *boom* echoed through the cavern, shaking the walls and raining rock pellets over our heads.

"What was that?" Cora asked, somewhere to my right.

"I don't know," Artan answered.

"I think it was the alchemists," Theron said.

"Yes, an alchemist bomb," Kane said from my left.

We didn't have time to muse over it as the battle went on. The number of red alchemists and revenants didn't seem to reduce at all. Either they were able to resurrect, or more were coming into the den.

Another boom shook the cavern, this time hard enough that I lost my balance and end up on one knee on the hard ground. But this time, the shaking didn't stop right away.

I pushed up and used my spell to decapitate two more revenants. Then the walls and ground shook, but this time, it wasn't from the bombs.

Shit.

Through here, Ramon called out in my mind. I glanced back and saw him at the doorway to another room, behind the log-like throne. *There's a passageway in here.*

What? He wanted to abandon the den? But as I looked around, I understood why. There was nothing here anymore. The werewolves had been evacuated, and the den was coming apart. The ground and the rock walls shook more and more, dropping small pellets over our heads. Soon, it wouldn't be small raindrops, but full-sized boulders.

There was nothing we could do for this place anymore.

Following Ramon's silent command, the remaining were-wolves turned and raced to the secret tunnel.

"Retreat," I called out, not too loud, so our enemies wouldn't be alerted.

After pushing their opponents away, or finishing them, my friends ran to the back. Artan hesitated, but after a grunt and an air punch, he joined us.

The room was small and tight, but people filtered through into a small hole in the opposite wall. I saw as Ellie, Kizzy, Cora, and Rye disappeared into it.

I stared at the door. The revenants and red alchemists advanced fast. "They are coming!"

The shelf, Ramon said to Theron and me. *That's why it's there.*

A heavy stone shelf rested beside the opening.

"Help," Theron said, grabbing the shelf. He pushed it, trying to make it fall over the opening.

Artan, Kane, and I pushed with all our might.

Wait ... I looked back at the tunnel. Felix, Vira, Violet, Ellie, Kizzy, Cora, and Rye had already gone through, and Ramon, Theron, Artan, and Kane were here with me.

Then, where was Trina?

Something tugged at my chest, and I turned to the doorway of the little room. Beyond the red alchemists and beyond the revenants, I could make out a delicate, wicked figure.

Damara.

And right beside her—Trina.

21

THE GUYS FINALLY TIPPED THE SHELF, AND IT FELL OVER THE opening, sealing us in the small room. They raced to the tunnel, disappeared into it.

And I didn't move.

I couldn't.

"Mirella?" Kane called. "What happened?"

I shook my head, sending the imagine etched in my mind away. "Nothing. Let's go."

I followed him into the tunnel, and while we ducked our heads in the winding, dark tunnel, my mind raced. It couldn't be. I had imagined Trina beside Damara. They were too far away, and with all the rock dust from the crumbling place, I couldn't identify the second person. She had looked like Trina. That had to be it.

But deep down, I knew it wasn't. I knew the woman standing beside Damara was Trina. I knew now what she was hiding, who she had been communicating with.

And I felt so stupid, so betrayed.

We raced through the tunnels for almost an hour, until

finally we emerged at the base of the mountain, miles away from the den. I blinked against the brightness of the sun, which had started its descent.

Sundown.

Go to Lovell.

That was still the plan, wasn't it?

My friends got together to the side of the tunnel, sitting down on rocks and catching their breaths. The werewolves gathered on the other side, all of them shifting back to their human forms, and tending to the ones who had gotten hurt while fleeing.

"How did she find out where we were?" Cora asked, repeating Theron's earlier question.

I approached them, my eyes on the ground. "It was Trina."

"What?" Kane asked, in shock.

Everyone looked around, searching for her.

"I saw her with Damara a few seconds before you sealed the passage."

"She could have been captured, right?" Ellie asked.

I shook my head. "She stood beside Damara, free, casual. As if they were friends. Or allies."

Kizzy gasped, her hands over her mouth. "She betrayed us."

I nodded.

"Trina wouldn't do that," Kane muttered.

A little worm-sized jealousy slithered through my chest, because he seemed to care about her at this moment, but I knew where he was coming from. In all the time they were together, she might never have revealed this side of her to him. Spending a long time with someone and not really knowing them hurt. It hurt too much.

"I'm sorry," I whispered.

"This is your fault." Artan pointed to Kane. "You're the one who brought her to work with us."

What was up with Artan and blaming people? He was always the first to stand up and point fingers.

"I didn't know," Kane said quickly. "Before, she had never acted like that. She hadn't—"

"I think it's a recent thing," I said, coming up with that excuse to stop this stupid argument. "She might have been working with Damara already when Kane called her to help us, but he hadn't seen her in months. He didn't know her that well anymore. She could have changed a lot in that time." A long, loud breath escaped through my parted lips. "Regardless, there's nothing we can do about it now. She betrayed us. Now, we forget about her and move on."

"So we'll stick to the plan?" Theron asked. "We're going to the enclave right now?"

"If no one opposes that, I don't see why not," I said.

Rye cleared his throat. "This may sound a little crazy, but what if we go around the mountain and ambush Damara and her minions on the other side, at the den's main entrance? I'm sure her numbers have dwindled after our fight and hopefully more got stuck when the den came down. If we plan it right, this might be the best opportunity to hit her."

"By the time you get to the den's entrance, Damara will be long gone," Ramon said, joining us. He had a pair of ragged trousers on and nothing else.

"Where did you get those?" I asked in a low voice.

"Violet knew about these," he replied. "Apparently, there was a box filled with clothes and money outside the tunnel, in case something like this happened." He cleared his throat. "Anyway, the secret tunnel cut down through the mountain, sending us to the opposite side. To get to the den, you'll have to go up and around the mountain. The long way, if you will. It'll take several hours to get there."

"So, even if we wanted to go back and attack her, it wouldn't work," Cora stated.

Ramon shook his head. "Like I said, she'll be long gone by the time you get there."

"Then we have no other choice," Theron said. "We stick to the plan and go back to the enclave."

"I'm not going," Ramon declared.

"What? Why?" I asked, alarmed. He seemed so intent on helping out just a couple of hours earlier.

"My pack needs me now." He gestured to the people gathered a few feet from us. "We just lost our home, and we have a few injured wolves. I need to find a safe place for us to spend the night, and then I have to figure out the rest."

By Saint Sara-la-Kali, how could I have been so selfish?

"I'm sorry," I muttered. "If I hadn't dragged you into this—"

Ramon let out a hollow chuckle. "I think I sent my wolves to drag *you* here, not the other way around." His grin fell. "It's okay. Werewolves are resilient. We'll be okay."

"Thank you," I muttered. "For everything."

Ramon embraced me. "Right now, I'm going to focus on my wolves, but know this: I'm always here for you. Always."

I wound my arms around him tight. Then Theron threw himself over us. "Us too," Theron said. "If you need help, rebuilding your place or whatever, call us."

Ramon pulled back and offered us a sad smile. "I will." He took a step back and slipped his hand into Violet's. "Good luck."

"You too," Theron and I said in unison.

In silence, we watched as Ramon gathered his werewolves and guided them into the forest. Only when all of them had disappeared beyond the trees did I finally snap out of my trance.

I inhaled deeply, wiped the wetness from my eyes, and looked at my friends. "Who is ready for more?"

WE STOPPED ABOUT A MILE FROM THE ENCLAVE, HIDDEN BEHIND the trees, waiting as the sun descended behind the trees. Time seemed to slow down, as if teasing us, making us more tense and tired, even though we hadn't even started the battle yet.

Although I knew, I truly knew, we wouldn't be able to avoid some kind of physical confrontation, I wished with all my heart that Darcy and Oscar and the other elder members woke up from whatever darkness clouded their judgments and promised to do better, to be better. To fix the wrongs they had done, to be more lenient and helpful and caring. To help me while we all searched for a cure for the fire heart fever. To allow me to be a heart maiden for a long time so I could continue providing the heart flower to the enclave.

It was all a dream, a beautiful, perfect dream I clutched tight.

"As soon as the sun is down, we go," Artan said, taking the lead. When he was absent, Theron had become the leader of the warriors, but now we weren't even sure there were any warriors left to be leader of.

Beside me, Theron stiffened. I sensed he wanted to start an argument, telling Artan who was the leader here, but for the sake of the group, he decided to stay quiet.

In the end, it didn't matter who was the leader of our group, as long as we all fought together and remained together.

Tired of waiting, I stepped from behind the bushes. "This is stupid. We don't plan to attack, right? Not unless they attack first. Then, what are we waiting for? Let's move. The sooner we start this, the sooner it'll be done."

Kane was by my side in a second.

Artan furrowed, probably upset with the decision, but he was the next one to come out of hiding. "You're right. We should just go."

The others exchanged unsure glances, but didn't argue.

When my mother halted by my side, I hesitated. I opened my mouth to tell her to stay behind, but stopped myself. For so long, she had kept me in the dark, kept her secrets from me, so I would be safe. In the end, none of that mattered as I ended up in trouble anyway. Now, I was about to do the same with her. Tell her to stay behind so she would be safe.

No, I couldn't do that to her. She knew well the danger we were getting ourselves in and for once she didn't try to stop me. I wouldn't stop her either.

I slipped my hand in hers and squeezed tight. She turned alarmed eyes to me, but when she saw the small smile on my lips, she relaxed.

Side by side, my friends, my mother, and I walked toward the enclave's main gates—Felix and Vira at the ends.

As expected, the warriors guarding the gates saw us coming.

Tobbar appeared at the lookout above the wall. "Open the gates!" he shouted.

With a cringing groan, the gates opened, and a dozen warriors greeted us, their swords held high.

I held out my hands. "We've come in peace. All I want is to talk to the elder council."

The warriors looked at each other. Some whispers were exchanged. I was starting to doubt they would let us in when Tobbar finally spoke up. "You can come, but keep your hands where I can see them!" I took the first step past the gates. "And spread out! I don't want you all too close."

I dipped my chin once, telling my friends to do as we were asked. Soon, we marched through the streets of the enclave, spread out in two uneven lines, at least five feet from each other, flanked by not only the guards who had been at the gates, but another two dozen of them. Where the hell did Darcy get so many warriors? What did she offer the other enclaves to let her borrow them? What lies had she spun?

Slowly, the tziganes crawled out of their houses, curious about the commotion outside. They all seemed alarmed at seeing the heart maiden and Artan, their beloved warrior, escorted by several blades' edges to the center of the enclave.

At the square, Darcy, Oscar, and the other elder council members waited for us, right in front of the fountain, like she was a mob boss and the elders were her gangsters. Even Neil was with them, though he seemed unsure of what was going on. I always had my suspicion that Darcy had let Neil join the council when he moved from Bellville to Lovell, more out of show than anything else. And now, as he looked side to side, confused, I had an inkling he didn't know one tenth of what the council really did.

Darcy's eyes met mine, the ire and hate visible in their darkness. She then shifted her gaze to the crowd gathering around us. The entire enclave was here. In the back, I could even see Dolan, Sheila, Jayme, Leander and Lash, who had come out of hiding—I hoped Bryna, Marie, and Anne, and the kids were still hiding though since we didn't know how things would turn out here.

With a slight gesture from her hand, Darcy ordered the warriors to lower their swords. A moment later, they did, but their eyes didn't lose focus. One wrong movement, and I was sure they would strike us down, as they had been instructed.

"My dear friends," I spoke out loud, hoping my voice carried through the entire square. "We've looked up to the elder council for so long, we never questioned their good intentions. Unfortunately, I'm here to tell you about their evil ways."

Gasps spread through the crowd like wildfire.

Darcy advanced a step. "Mirella, I advise you to stop right now."

I ignored her and went on, "The elder council has been controlling every aspect of our lives. They want us to walk the line they draw, and if we waver, we're struck down. Recently, I was struck down. Seen as a threat to their ideals, I was captured and locked away in a hidden room underneath the infirmary. I was tortured and beaten and starved." I gestured to Kane a couple of feet behind me. "Master Slayer Kane was also there, chained to the ceiling and unconscious."

"No, it can't be."

"The elder council did that?"

"To the heart maiden? But why?"

The whispers and doubt grew.

I pointed at the old hag. "It was all ordered by Darcy. She was the one behind it all and the elder council simply agreed to it, making them accomplices."

"Lies!" Darcy shouted. Her hands curled at her sides, and I could see she was fighting to remain in control of herself. "Mirella is lying. You see, being a heart maiden has its downside. It brings a madness and makes her mind and magic unstable. Yes, I locked her away, but it was because she was starting to hurt others. It was for her own good."

"You tortured me!"

"That's what you think," Darcy said, nonchalantly. "You were deep in your madness and your mind created scenes that didn't really happen."

Oh, she was trying to pin this one me, the old hag. My power awoke inside me, but I pushed it down. I had been the one to instigate a peaceful understanding, wasn't I? I wouldn't charge on her, though she clearly deserved it, unless she came for me first.

"Darcy is lying," I snarled.

"As you can see, Mirella is mad. Her mind doesn't work well anymore, thus, she is no longer fit to be the heart maiden."

I blinked. Was she really saying that? "No longer fit to be the heart maiden? That's not for you to decide."

"Mirella is the best heart maiden this enclave ever had," Cora said.

Darcy glared at her. "How do you know? You weren't alive when the last heart maiden was here and you aren't even from our enclave."

Cora flinched.

"But we do know the last heart maiden," Theron said. "We know Damara and she's evil."

Whispers rose among the crowd. The tziganes still hadn't heard about Damara being alive and fighting against us, and now they murmured about what the hell we were talking about.

"Just like you!" Kizzy shouted above the whispers.

"Mirella has done so much for us," Rye said. "She found

the heart flower and made the heart elixir when we needed it the most."

"She went after the alchemists and got us back from those revenants," Theron added.

"She defied you and made the elixir that saved the soulless tziganes," Ellie said.

"She restored the land and brought back spring," Kane said.

My heart swelled as their words reached me. My friends pointing out all the good I had done in the past few months was the best thing I had heard in awhile. For someone who often thought she wasn't worthy of being the heart maiden, I guess I did well enough.

I did my best.

I would always to my best.

"That was before!" Darcy's voice grew louder. More desperate. "Before you became truly mad." She looked out to the confused tziganes. "Mirella can't be trusted anymore. We need to think about what's good for this enclave, for all enclaves, for all tziganes," she said, regaining some of her composure. "What is better: deal with a mad heart maiden or take her aside and wait for a new one?"

I hadn't heard her right. "Are you suggesting ..."

"A new heart maiden will only be born after the previous one dies." The corner of her mouth curled up slightly.

Goose bumps rolled up my arms. And she was saying I was the mad one.

A new wave of gasps washed over the tziganes.

"*Puri daj*," Artan said, his voice low but powerful among us. "Please, stop."

"I'm trying to keep this peaceful," I warned her. "Please, step down before we remove you by force."

Her eyes on mine, Darcy pointed her index finger at me. "Warriors, take the heart maiden and her friends." A couple of warriors raised their swords right away, some hesitated, their hands shaking, and others stepped back. "What are you doing? Take them!"

"It seems we'll have to fight," Kane said.

My heart sank. "I didn't want it to end like this."

I called on my magic.

"Take them!" Darcy shouted.

The warriors, more out of fear than anything, advanced on us.

I lifted my hands, ready to strike them, when I was pulled back. Tziganes swarmed my friends and me, pushing us back, until we were in the center of a thick ring of tziganes.

A lot of tziganes.

And they were all standing between Darcy and me.

"You can't take them," Sheila said.

Lost, Darcy stared at the crowd. Even her granddaughter, Ryane, stood among us. I suspected the few tziganes who remained still, away from us, were simply afraid of Darcy's wrath, not because they believed her.

It didn't matter. Darcy wouldn't hurt us while so many of her people stood between us, with so many of them protecting me.

I was wrong.

The air crackled as Darcy channeled her power. "Attack!"

22

LIKE A TRULY CRAZY OLD HAG, DARCY THREW A STRIKE IN MY direction—a jet of water, transformed into thin shards of ice —and the direction of at least three tziganes who stood between us.

With barely a moment to spare, I pulled them back and raised a thin fire wall, just enough to take her hit.

"Are you okay?" I asked them. Faces pale and eyes wide, they nodded. Yeah, I was sure seeing the woman who was supposed to be a bigger voice than even the *rom baro* trying to kill them was a shock. "Just ... stay out of the way."

Another strike hit the wall, breaking it and sending sparks of fire through the air.

I stared at the old hag. Shit, she was powerful.

And just like that, a civil war started. Darcy, Oscar, the elder council, the visitor from other enclaves, and two thirds of the warriors against the rest of us—most of the Lovell tziganes, my friends and family, and me.

To my relief, Neil stepped away from the council and joined us, standing with Sheila and Dolan and my mother.

More than ever, I really doubted he had ever agreed or known what was really going on, since he was a Bellville tzigane at the core, but I was glad when he broke the facade and ditched them.

Darcy didn't see his betrayal. In fact, I didn't think she saw anything in front of her as she struck everyone in her path. I kept lifting shields to absorb her attacks, trying to keep the innocents from being hurt.

"Get back!" I shouted. "Please, get out of the way!"

Only a handful of tziganes listened to me and chose to retreat and hide. The others stayed by my side, by my friends' side, their legs apart and hands up, ready to take any hit.

With a crazed glint to her eyes that reminded me of Damara, Darcy threw a strike at a scared teenager. I tried getting to her before the hit landed on her, but I was too far away from her. Thankfully, Artan appeared by her side, and using his air magic, deflected the hit upward. It exploded in tiny sparkling shards that rained down over our heads.

"*Puri daj.*" Hands raised, Artan stepped toward his grandmother. "Please stop this." She glanced at him, but she looked like a caged animal. She didn't truly see him, and if she did, then she didn't know who he was. Artan let out a shuddering breath. "Please, *puri daj*, this isn't you."

"Get out of my way!" She waved her hand, sending a strike directly to him. Artan was able to absorb most of the impact with his magic, but Darcy succeeded in pushing him aside.

Like a maniac, she rushed into the crowd.

I went after her, but had to stop and deflect a sword swing before it slashed an innocent tzigane in half. I knocked the warrior's sword to the ground and pressed my hand to his chest, sending my fire into him. He gasped as the fire warmed his insides and stunned him. Unconscious but alive, he fell to the ground.

I looked around, searching for Darcy, and saw my friends. Artan now screamed at Oscar in a heated argument, Kizzy beside him. Cora, Rye, Jayme, Leander, and Lash engaged the warriors, trying to put them down without actually hurting them. Theron did the same, but he guided the tziganes who wanted out of the fight toward Ellie, who was helping them hide. Felix and Vira were constantly swarmed by warriors, but they linked their minds and used their magic to push them away.

This sight, tziganes fighting against tziganes, broke my heart. When and how did we get here? It didn't matter now, because I would fix it all. Somehow.

When I caught sight of Darcy again, she was in the middle of the crowd, dropping tziganes left and right. I really hoped she wasn't killing anyone.

I weaved past the tziganes, avoiding the warriors who came for me, and got closer to Darcy.

My eyes were set on her when she lifted her arm and threw her magic out. The shard zipped through the air.

Directly toward my mother.

"No!" I screamed, though with the loud clank of swords and hiss of strikes and groans and yelps, I doubted anyone had heard me.

Dolan pushed my mother to the side, but the razor-sharp shard grazed her shoulder.

Red. All I saw in front of me was red.

Darcy was as good as dead.

Channeling my magic, I marched to her and grabbed her neck. My hand turned orange and Darcy gasped.

"Mirella, no." Kane hooked his arm around my waist.

Dolan caught my arm and pulled it back. "Mi, stop it."

They pulled me back until Darcy was free from my grasp. I thrashed against them.

"Mi, look at me." Kane cupped my cheek with one of his big hands and turned my face so my nose was less than an inch from his. "This isn't you. You're better than this. You're the heart maiden, the best one yet." He smoothed his thumb over my cheek. "Fight the madness." I stared at him, lost in the green flecks in his hazel eyes. Beautiful. Ensnaring. Grounding. I took a long breath and let go of my magic. "There you are."

"Thank you," I whispered.

He rested his forehead against mine. "Always."

The horror of the situation came rushing back to me. I pulled back, glancing back at Darcy. Only, she wasn't there anymore. Holding my rage in check, I turned to my mother. "Are you okay?"

She had a hand pressed against her shoulder. "Yes, it hurts a little, but it was just a scratch. I'll be fine."

Dolan stepped beside her. "Don't worry. I'll take care of her."

I dipped my chin in acknowledgement, then looked around for Darcy again.

"There," I said, pointing at her. She was almost at the other side of the enclave, among other elder council members, clearly trying to escape. "Stop!" I shouted. "Stop them!"

My friends turned toward Darcy and the council, intent on stopping them.

But when we got close, they grabbed innocent tziganes.

"Stay back!" Darcy cried. "Or we'll hurt them!"

By Saint Sara-la-Kali, they were using the tziganes as shields. Like this, they knew we wouldn't strike against them.

Rage came back when I saw who Darcy had in her arms.

Ryane. Her granddaughter. The young woman cried as she begged her grandmother to let her go, but Darcy either didn't hear her or she didn't care. In truth, I thought Darcy was so out of it, she didn't realize the one she was threatening was her own flesh and blood.

I stopped a way away from them. Each time someone thought about going after Darcy and the others, I stopped them.

"What do we do?" Theron asked, standing by my side, his gaze trained on the retreating traitors.

"Just don't attack them," Artan said from beside him. "That's my sister."

"I know, but we can't let them go either," Kane said.

He was right, of course, but how could we stop them without risking innocent tziganes?

My only idea was to raise a wall of fire behind them, sealing the exit, but then I would have to do that with all the exits and keep the wall up until they gave in and let the tziganes go, and only Saint Sara-la-Kali knew how much longer they could fight us.

If I had to keep the wall up for long, I would be drained quickly.

I felt them before they showed up by my side.

Felix and Vira flanked me, sending an image to my mind.

Following their lead, I placed my hand on top of their heads. Instantly, their magic flowed into me, strong, powerful, pure. Just as strong as the fire well inside me.

With our joined magic, I lifted fire walls all around the square, sealing us all in a tall ring of fire. A smile spread across my lips as I realized that, this way, I wouldn't need to keep the wall up by myself. The heart animals could do it, while I use my power for something else.

Like stopping the elder council once and for all.

I looked at Darcy. "Looks like you're trapped."

23

Slowly, I raised my hands in a peace sign and took a step forward. "Please, let them go."

Darcy squeezed Ryane's throat. "Die first! Kill yourself. Then I'll let them go."

She had truly lost it. But ... had she lost it a few minutes ago when this battle started, or had she gone mad long ago?

"Darcy—"

"Please," Ryane croaked.

My heart tugged. I had to do something.

With a half-assed plan hashed out in my mind, I took another step closer to the council. "Darcy," I tried again. "Hear me out."

"Now!" Darcy screamed.

Boldo, one of the oldest council members, let go of the tzigane he had been holding and raised a dome of white light around them. Around me.

I was trapped inside the dome with the elder council members.

Shit.

"Mirella!" Kane rushed to the shield, but when he tried touching it, a zap came out of it, pushing him away.

I stared at him as he wobbled back, holding his hand. Theron and Kizzy hovered over him, making sure he was all right.

I turned my enraged eyes to Darcy. "By Saint Sara-la-Kali, you're testing my patience."

Cackling like a mad woman, Darcy let go of Ryane. "My dear, we haven't even started yet."

The other elders let go of their hostages, and they huddled on one side of the dome, afraid of the people they had once looked up to.

"All right, Darcy, this is over," I said, channeling my power. "Drop the shield and surrender."

"Why would I when we can finally have fun?" At that, she threw her magic at me.

I easily sidestepped the hit. "This is—"

Another strike came at me and I dodged it too. She send three more hits and I lagged, almost not moving out of the way fast enough. If she kept that up, I would soon be hit. It was that, or move more, which meant risking the other tziganes getting hit. No, I would rather get hit myself.

"Shall we up the ante?" Darcy teased. What the hell did she mean? "Now," she whispered.

The other council members threw their magic at me.

I raised a shield of fire before me. The hits bumped against the shield, strong and stronger.

Behind me, my family and friends attacked the dome, trying to break it somehow.

"Hang on," Kane said, a desperate edge to his voice. "We'll find a way to get to you."

I sent more of my magic to my shield, but the elders hit it all at once. The fire crackled and went up in smoke. I called for another wall, but before I could get a grip on my mind, several bolts hit me.

"Mirella!" my mother shouted.

I fought against them, I tried to resist them, but each time their magic hit me, it drained me of mine. Pain spread, my vision blurred, my muscles went slack, and I fell to my knees. The bolts hit me square in the chest, taking my breath away.

Then pain started at the back of my mind.

The madness.

Somehow the magical dome was blocking my connection to Kane and the madness had a hold on me.

Without a choice, I didn't resist it. Instead, I dove into it.

A scream ripped past my throat as I stood. The magic continued to slam at me, but I no longer hurt. I no longer felt it.

My fire rolled inside my veins, like a tsunami ready to destroy towns. Strong and proud, I spread my legs apart and raised my hands. Fire arced out of my hands, washing over the council members.

Although, somehow, I had a grip on my madness and despite its will to kill, I reined it in. Instead of letting the full blow of my power hit them, I sent the fire to numb them. Then, snakes of fire fell to the ground and rolled themselves up the limp bodies of the elder council members, tying them tight. If one struggled against it, the fire heated up, burning them until they stopped.

Boldo fainted and the domed faded away.

The magic and the pain screamed inside me, and I dropped to my knees again, tired of fighting, without one ounce of strength.

"Mirella!" I heard someone calling, but I wasn't sure who.

I blinked as the madness retreated. The pain in my skull faded and my vision cleared. But my body told me otherwise.

Blackness surrounded me, and I didn't even try to fight it.

24

IF I FAINTED, IT WAS ONLY FOR A SECOND. BEFORE I HIT THE ground, someone cradled my head. "Mirella, look at me." I blinked, trying to focus my sight. A handsome and sharp face appeared right in front of me. "You're all right." Kane embraced me. "By Saint Sara-la-Kali, you gave me quite the scare."

"I'm fine." Tired, hurting, but fine. I clutched him. "Help me up."

"Mirella." My mother was over me the next second, and right behind her, I could see the worried gazes of Dolan, Sheila, Theron, Ellie, and everyone else. "Are you all right? Are you hurt?"

"I'll be fine," I muttered, my focus on the tziganes, who stared at the scene, still too shocked to breathe right.

Some dared get closer to the elder council members, mostly family members. They knelt beside their loved ones and asked why. Why they had done that.

"What are we going to do with them?" Theron asked, eyeing the elders.

"We'll lock them away, in some kind of jail," I said, though I wouldn't use the jails or hidden rooms they had put me in. I would find a way to have them more comfortable than that, though I wasn't sure they deserved it, like an enchanted house where they would be okay inside, but couldn't leave. "We'll figure something out."

"The people look distraught," my mother said.

Kane tugged at my hand. "Maybe you should talk to them."

He was right. The enclave was in chaos, the elder council was gone, and everyone looked lost. As the heart maiden, I had to help them feel at ease.

With Kane's help, I stepped onto the fountain's ledge. "Can I have your attention, please?"

Murmurs spread through the square, until everyone realized what was going on and turned to face me. I gulped, suddenly conscious that some people here were hurt, or angry, or lost, and it was my job to help them, to guide them. My heart pounded against my chest. Sometimes, I really wasn't sure I was cut out to be the heart maiden they deserved.

"What happens now?" someone asked.

I cleared my throat. "Now, we begin anew." The murmurs stopped and the tziganes fell silent. "The previous council used to manipulate us, and they weren't afraid of hurting us. I guarantee you, the new council won't."

The murmurs and whispers were back.

"New council?"

"Who will they be?"

"Do we have enough elders?"

"I wouldn't want to be on the council."

"This time," I spoke louder, cutting them off. "The council

won't be comprised of only elders. Times are changing, and changing fast, and even though we'll always honor tradition and respect our elders, we don't want to be left behind. I know it sounds scary, but we need to change too." I gestured to my family and friends standing right in front of me. "For the new council, I appoint Marisa, Dolan, Sheila, Theron, Ellie, Artan, Kizzy, Rye, Cora, and Kane." They all stared at me, surprised. "Please, be assured that I'll always work alongside them to ensure all your problems are heard and fixed. We will restore the greatness of the Lovell and the Bellville enclaves, together, and begin a new era of peace."

I expected lots of protests, but instead heard sentences I wasn't expecting.

"They have been by the heart maiden's side all along."

"They went on many missions together."

"They work well together."

"They saved us many, many times."

"But there's a human in the middle."

"Why is a human among them?"

"I'm inviting a human to the council because of the change I just said," I cut the whispers off before they instigate more revolt. "She has been through a lot with us, she knows us and our customs, and she understand us. If we are to accept change, we need diversity, and Ellie can offer that to us." I saw lots of heads bouncing up and down in agreement.

"Who will be the new *rom baro*?" someone asked.

Good question. I hadn't thought of that. Now that Oscar had been detained with Darcy and the rest of the elder council, we didn't have a *rom baro* anymore.

Shit.

I cleared my throat, thinking fast. "We'll worry about a *rom baro* later. Because right now, we have more important things to worry about. The real war isn't over yet. Damara is coming for us and we need to be prepared."

"What do you mean, Damara?"

"The heart maiden?"

"But she's dead!"

It was time they knew. "A few months ago, we learned that Damara faked her death. Using the power of the heart flower, she was able to keep herself alive for over two hundred years. However, taking in so much power had a downside. She went mad. Her mind is lost to revenge and evil. She is working with alchemists and revenants and is preparing for a war to kill all of us." Gasps of shock were quickly followed by mutters of horrors. "But rest assured, we're working on stopping her," I continued, my voice louder. "We'll take the rest of the night off to rest and process all of the sudden changes, but tomorrow morning, we'll gather in the council room for a meeting where I'll have tasks for each one of you. Everyone will participate in the final battle." Some tziganes looked excited to be included, and some looked afraid. I didn't care about that right now. Tomorrow I could explain to the fearful ones how important their participation was, but for now, I wanted a few hours of quiet and peace. "Go. Rest. Meet us tomorrow at eight in the council room."

I stepped off the ledge.

"Are you crazy?" Cora was the first to ask. "Me? A council member?"

I looked from her to all my friends gathered around me. "You heard them. We have been through a lot together. They trust us. *I* trust us. Just follow your heart and we'll be fine. But for now ..." I stared at Artan. "Please, take a few of your trusted warriors, if we still have those, and make sure the perimeter is secured so we won't have any surprises tonight."

He dipped his chin and marched away. Next was Theron and Rye. "You two, please, escort the visiting enclaves and warriors out. I want them gone within the hour."

"You got it," Theron said before turning and following with his task with Rye.

Then, I pointed to Kane, Dolan, and Cora. "You will help me take the council members and the treacherous warriors to someplace safe for tonight. Tomorrow we worry about where they will stay."

Dolan nodded. "Sounds good." He started toward the elders, still bound and numb on the stone pavement. Cora followed him.

"What about me?" my mother asked.

"And me?" Ellie and Kizzy asked in unison.

I smiled. "I'm really hungry. If you can get some dinner ready for us, we'll meet you back at my mother's house. Okay?"

They all agreed and left for their tasks.

Kane snaked his arm around my shoulders and tugged me to his side. "I loved seeing you taking charge, so sure of yourself. It is pretty hot."

Fighting a smile, I rolled my eyes at him. "Save it—" I gestured to his face—his eyes were glued to mine and shining with pure desire. "—for later, okay? Now come help me."

He leaned into me and placed a kiss on the top of my head. "Yes, ma'am."

***

IN THE END, WE TOOK THE PREVIOUS COUNCIL MEMBERS TO JAIL —I couldn't think of a better place since we would need time to set up something better, and I told myself they deserved to stay in a rough place for a couple of days. It wouldn't be a big deal.

After we were done, Dolan and Cora went to check on Felix and Vira, making sure their cage was clean and they had enough food for now. Then they would go to my mother's house. Meanwhile Kane and I walked around the enclave, making sure everything else was all right. Besides a couple of tziganes returning to their homes for the night, we didn't encounter any problems or worrying matters.

But because of our patrol, it was almost midnight when we finally joined the others at my mother's. The place was full, but not as much as I thought it would be. Because of the time, Marie had already taken Anne to their place, same with Jayme, Bryna, and their baby.

Rye and Cora sat side-by-side on one of the loveseats, full plates in their laps. Theron and Ellie were at the table beside the kitchen with Kizzy, Ryane, and Thomas. Artan stood by the wall a couple of feet behind them, always quiet and paying attention. Sheila and Dolan were in the kitchen with my mother, helping her with dessert, while Neil stood to the side, also quiet, but for an entirely different reason.

From what Dolan had told me while we locked the council members away, Neil didn't know about half of what the council was doing, and he really didn't know that they had me locked up and tortured. Seeing as he was my uncle, he felt guilty.

I approached him, standing by his side. "I know you didn't have a hand in any of that."

He stared straight ahead as he said, "It doesn't change the fact that you were being hurt right under my nose."

I rested a hand on his upper arm. "I don't hold anything against you, so you shouldn't either."

He shifted his gaze to mine, pain stamped as clear as day. "For what it is worth, I really am sorry."

I offered him a small smile. "Thank you." I stepped away from him and walked over to my mother and Sheila. I sniffed the chocolatey scent coming from the pot in front of them and sighed. "I think I'm skipping dinner and eating whatever that is."

My mother elbowed me in the stomach. "No, you won't. Eat a full plate. Get some energy back. Then I'll let you eat as much dessert as you want."

"I'm not five anymore, you know that, right?"

She faked a loud gasp. "You aren't?" I pouted but I couldn't hold it and ended up chuckling at my stupid attempt to make myself more childish. She slapped my arm, but ended up turning around and taking me in her arms. "I'm very proud of you," she whispered in my ear.

"Thank you," I whispered back.

Sheila held up a plate full of goulash right in front of my face. "Your mother is right. You need sustenance."

I disentangled myself from my mother and took the plate. "*Nais tuke.*"

Two steps from me, Kane stood, holding a similar plate, probably given to him by Sheila too.

We took places at the table with the others and dug in. A moment later, I was coughing, startled by how spicy the food was. I glanced at my mother and Sheila, and they were bickering about the dessert. They probably went overboard with the goulash too and ended up putting in more pepper and other spicy things than usual.

"It's a little hot," Kane said, stifling a cough.

I looked around. Everyone was drinking juice and soda

and sweet tea, but right now, I wanted something simpler. "I'll get some water." I started pushing my chair back.

"Wait." Kizzy's hand shot across the table. "I was about to get up to get water for myself. I'll get it for you too."

"Oh." I stared at her. "Are you sure?"

She flashed a big smile at me. "Absolutely." She shot up and raced to the fridge.

Beside me, Kane pulled my chair closer. "I want you right by my side."

My chair touched his and I scooted to the edge, so my leg was pressed against his. "Like this?"

He leaned over me. "It'll be better later." He brushed his lips against mine.

Usually, I would be freaking out about PDA and other people seeing a man touching me, because, holy shit, I was the damn heart maiden, but I didn't care about any of that right now.

I sighed against his mouth.

"Here you go!" Kizzy placed two water bottles in front of us. Kane and I glanced at her as she sat down, smiling. She opened the water bottle she had brought for herself. "Oh, you can keep doing whatever you were doing. Sorry to interrupt." She winked at us.

Warmth spread through my cheeks and inevitably, my gaze found Artan's a few steps back. Contrary to his wife, he glared at us—at me. What? Was I bothering him? Really?

Suddenly upset, I reached for my water bottle.

A coughing fit took over Kizzy and she dropped her water bottle, spilling the water all over the table. Her hands trembled and soon her body shook.

Artan rushed to her. "Kizzy!" He cradled her in his arms,

as the tremors became stronger and her muscles locked. "What is happening? Kizzy!"

He lowered her to the ground as Ryane shot to his side. "Let me see."

We all gathered around them, watching as Kizzy trembled uncontrollably and Ryane tried to find whatever was wrong and heal her. Her eyes were wide and foam formed at her mouth.

"The water!" Theron pointed to the water bottle in my hand. I hadn't even noticed I was still holding the damn bottle. "It's the water."

Kane grabbed the bottle from me and opened it. He sniffed the liquid and wrinkled his nose. "It's poison."

Artan's face paled. "W-what?"

Ryane cursed. "I can't treat her here. We have to take her to the infirmary."

Artan gathered Kizzy in his arms.

But the next second, she locked eyes with him and let out a groan. Then, her head rolled back and her body went limp.

Kizzy was dead.

25

T HE NEXT FEW HOURS WERE A BLUR. W ITH THE HELP OF A RTAN
and Thomas, Ryane took Kizzy's body to the infirmary, where
they could fully examine it and prepare it for a funeral the
next day.

Theron left soon after, saying something about checking
on Artan, and Rye and Cora excused themselves, probably to
go back to the Bellville house, where they could pretend
tragedy hadn't struck us again.

Leaning against the kitchen island, I pressed the heels of
my hands to my eyes, tired and sad and angry.

"I think I'm done," Kane announced. He had been exam-
ining the water in all of the bottles inside the fridge right in
my mother's kitchen.

I looked up, curious. "And?"

"The poison is an alchemist's work, for sure." His tone
was hard, guarded.

Seated beside me, Ellie gasped. "No."

"So, you mean ..." I sucked in a sharp breath. "It was
Trina?"

Kane shrugged. "Who else?"

I glanced back at my mother, who was seated at the table with Dolan and Sheila. "Did you see Trina here? Before you went to meet us?"

She started shaking her head, but then she paused. "Well, I've seen many of your friends inside the house, all the time, but I remember a couple of times Trina was here alone and she always told me she was looking for you. I never doubted that."

"You're saying she left that poisoned water there for us to drink?" Dolan asked.

Kane shook his head. "Not us." His gaze shifted to mine. "For Mirella."

My stomach revolved and nausea threatened to spill the contents of my dinner all over the island. Because Kane was probably right. The poison had been intended for me, and Kizzy, a pure and innocent soul, had died in my place.

"But when did Trina do it?" Ellie asked. "Weren't you guys hiding in here while we were out?"

My mother shook her head. "No, we were all gathered at the Bellville house. Not here."

"She could have come here while we were out," Kane said.

More knots spread through my stomach. "I actually saw her sneaking out one night." Only Saint Sara-la-Kali knew how many more times she did that.

"Her intention was to lead Damara to us," Kane mused. "But this would be plan B in case that failed. After all, she knew we planned on coming back."

The front door opened and we all jumped, startled by the loud noise. Theron stepped into the kitchen and all eyes were on him. "What happened?" he asked, frozen in place.

"How's Artan?" I asked. I couldn't stop the guilt that spread through me. The poison had been for me, and it had taken his wife instead. It seemed like a bad joke.

Theron shook his head. "Not well. He locked himself inside his house and is refusing to let anyone in." He let out a long breath. "To be honest, I'm afraid he might do something stupid."

Ellie shot up. "Then we won't leave him alone."

"I tried getting in by force, but he blasted me out with his wind," Theron said. "Believe me, I wouldn't mind spending the night there, making sure he's okay, but I can't fight his power, not unless I take him down, and I would rather not do that right now."

From what Theron was telling us, Artan was spiraling into a deep depression that would probably make him reckless and destructive.

I didn't even feel myself rising to my feet. "I'll go see him," I muttered.

Brows curled down, Kane looked at me. "Are you sure?"

"If he's not talking to Theron, then he won't talk to anyone else," I said.

"But you," Theron finished for me. "I think he would let you in and talk to you."

"Then you have to go," my mother said. She stood and rushed to the kitchen. "Here." She got a plate and filled it with dessert. "He might not feel like eating right now, but make sure that he sees the food there. He'll be hungry later." She shoved the plate in my hands.

Sheila brought over aluminum foil and covered the plate. "Tell him he doesn't have to endure this alone. He can come here and we'll keep him company."

"I will." I looked around at the others in the kitchen. "Any other messages?"

"Just tell him to let me in," Theron said. "I will be quiet and unmovable like a statue if he wants me to, but I just want to be there."

I nodded. "All right. Hopefully, I'll be back soon with him."

I caught Kane's eyes and he nodded, before following me to the foyer. He paused in front of the closed door, his body rigid, his brows still down. "Mirella—"

"Before you say anything, let me just explain. Someone needs to check on him and make sure he's okay and—"

"I know," he interrupted me, his voice heavy. "I know you're doing this out of the goodness of your heart. I bet you would go see whoever it is, not just Artan." He reached over and brushed a loose curl behind my ear. "I trust you. That's all that matters."

I smiled at him, proud of him. Of us. I had never met anyone like him before, and I couldn't believe how lucky I was. I stood on my tiptoes and pressed a quick kiss on his lips. "I'll be back soon."

He opened the door for me and closed it after I had walked by.

The enclave was quiet and eerie at this time of the night, and a painful pang cut through my heart when I realized almost no one knew Kizzy had died. In the morning, they would all know about it.

Would they blame me, like I blamed myself? The poison had been meant for me; we were positive of it. And yet, a pure, innocent soul had been claimed by it.

Tears brimmed my eyes. When all the death and pain and

battles would end? When would we be able to breathe without being afraid of being hurt?

Tziganes were such rare and powerful creatures. Unless we eliminated all alchemists, all revenants, all of our enemies from the entire world, there would always be a threat hanging over our heads.

I paused in front of the door to Artan's house. He lived in a large townhouse much like all the other houses in the enclave, along with his father, grandmother, and sister. I glanced at it. The lights were all out, which was normal for this time of the night, but more than before, I knew it was because Darcy and Oscar were in jail, Ryane was at the infirmary watching over Kizzy's body, and Artan was in here. Alone.

I knocked on the door.

The seconds ticked by and there was no answer, no sound.

I knocked again. "Artan. It's me." I wanted to yell to make sure he would hear me, but I didn't want to wake up the neighbors. "Please, open the door."

More seconds crawled by. I lifted my hand, ready to knock on the door, more forcefully this time, when I heard the clicking sound of the lock turning. The knob was next.

The door flew open, like magic.

Artan was sprawled on the stairs across the hallway, a glass and a bottle of whiskey beside him—two thirds of the amber liquid gone.

He waved his hand at me and a gentle wind blew behind my back, pushing me in. The moment I stepped inside, he sent the wind to push the door close. The lock clicked into place again.

"You shouldn't be here," he snarled, his words slurred from all the alcohol he consumed.

"Someone should." I approached him, a little worried about his drunkenness. What if he tried to hurt me? To hurt himself?

"Not you."

"Well, you weren't opening the door to anyone else."

He stared at me, and even through the darkness of the foyer, I could see his swollen, red eyes shooting daggers at me. "You shouldn't have come."

I set the plate with food on the end table along the wall and approached him. "Don't shut down. Let it all out. It'll be better for you."

He snorted and reached for the whiskey bottle. "You do not want me to let it all out."

I stared at the bottle as he tipped it over and drank several gulps. I wanted to snatch it away from him, but I didn't think opposing everything he was doing or saying would get me any points right now. I had to be understanding. Gentle. Caring.

"Artan ..."

He sprang to his feet, wobbling a little at the steps, but that didn't make me feel any more intimidated by his full height looming over me or his deadly gaze. "Don't Artan me! This is all your fault!"

My breath caught. Why the hell did he blame me for everything since we broke up? He didn't mind being verbal about it, and right now, scary too.

"Artan, please, calm down."

"Calm down? Calm down!" He advanced on me. "Since you came into my life, everything has gone wrong. I was fine marrying Kizzy until you showed up and I fell for you. After that, everything has been pain and suffering."

I backed away a couple of steps. "But ... you married her. I thought you loved her."

He snickered. "Loved her? No. I liked her well enough to give our doomed relationship a try, because it seemed I didn't have another choice." Artan thumped his chest with his closed fist. "And that's what hurts the most. I'm here mourning her as if I really loved her."

"Perhaps you did love her, you just—"

"I have only loved you!" His voice escalated and I flinched. "I still love you. And now I feel guilty and crazy and like a terrible man for having lost my wife, for hurting because she's gone. But do you know that after the shock was gone what the first thing that crossed my mind was?" I didn't dare answer, not only because I didn't know the answer, but because whatever I said would only make him madder. "I thought that now I am free. There is nothing stopping me from being with you. Only, there is!" He threw the bottle of whiskey on the wall, and I jumped, scared and shocked, as it broke in a million pieces and the remaining liquid splashed across the floor. "That damn master slayer showed up and he stole you from me."

I shook my head. I wanted to argue with him that he was wrong. Kane hadn't stolen me from Artan. Artan had thrown me aside, and I had let him go before Kane showed up, before Kane showed me how much he loved me and I found out I loved him too.

"Artan, please, take a deep breath." Hands raised, I took another step back, aiming for the door. I didn't want to leave him alone like this, but I wasn't sure staying was the best idea either. I would leave and send Theron back. He had to be the one to come and watch over Artan, even if he had to break down the door to do so. "Try to calm down."

He rushed me and I retreated, pressing my back on the closed door. "I'm not calming down." He slapped the door above my head, caging me in. I wrinkled my nose at his whiskey stench. "I don't want to calm down."

Very, very drunk, Artan swayed to the side. Without thinking, I reached to him, clasping his waist and trying to keep him from falling.

But Artan read something else in that gesture.

In a flash, he cradled my head with one of his hands and slammed his mouth down on mine.

Groaning, I pushed him away. "What the hell are you doing?"

As if I hadn't rejected him, Artan cupped my face with both hands and kissed me again. For a moment, one brief moment, guilt over his feelings, over the way he was mourning Kizzy while still loving me, made me pause. For that brief moment, I didn't push him away. To be honest, the guilt was so powerful, I even moved my lips with his.

But it wasn't right. He had lost his wife and he was too drunk to think straight. Tomorrow, he would wake up and regret having forcefully kissed me.

And there was Kane. I loved Kane more than I had ever loved anyone else in my life, past and present. Kane had been already through so much because of betrayal; I couldn't do this to him, even if this kiss didn't really mean anything.

As gentle as I could, I pushed Artan away.

When he didn't budge, I pressed my hands to his chest and called my fire. My hands warmed, and a moment later, he jumped back.

"What the ...?" He swayed again.

This time, I didn't reach for him, lest he think I was holding on to him again.

He fell hard on the floor, over most of the broken shards and the spilled whiskey. He groaned and scooted away a little, his hands red from the glass scratches. Artan leaned his back against the stairs, his eyes lolling into the back of his head. When I thought he was passed out, I knelt beside him and used some of my warmth to calm him down, to even his breathing, and take some of the upcoming headache and nausea away. He could use a peaceful sleep right now.

Since he was too heavy for me, I grabbed a pillow and a throw blanket from the living room and made him a little more comfortable on the cold wooden steps.

He rolled on his side, already fast asleep.

Like this, he looked like a lost boy.

Tears brimmed in my eyes.

Our love story had begun so beautiful and hopeful, and now it lay at our feet, the millions of pieces being carried away by the wind. Many of them already lost to time and space.

In my heart, I was sure of my love for Kane, but that didn't erase my past and didn't make seeing Artan in this state any easier.

But I wasn't anything of his anymore, and I didn't have the heart or gut to play his babysitter.

With a sigh, I stood and marched out of that house.

26

I DIDN'T GO BACK TO MY MOTHER'S HOUSE RIGHT AWAY. AT first, I walked around the quiet, dark enclave aimlessly.

Until I found myself in front of my abandoned cabin. How long had it been since I had stepped foot in there? But something else was calling me more than my warm bed.

I hiked down the valley behind my cabin and stopped near the lake around the waterfall.

The moon shone bright against the water, making it look white instead of dark blue. With the music of the waterfall filling my ears, I opened my arms and took a deep breath, trying to calm my thoughts and my hurting heart.

Why was I feeling so confused, so hurt? Yes, Kizzy had died and it had been because of me, but there was more to it.

In the end, I had to admit to myself. I was afraid of going back to my mother's house and facing Kane. When he married Trina, it hadn't been for love, but he had tried to be the best husband he could and he honestly hoped love would come for the both of them. It came, but not in the way he expected. Trina cheated on him, thus breaking his heart and his trust.

The fact that he had fallen for me as fast as I had fallen for him, and trusted me, and opened up to me, was a big thing, one I couldn't ignore. Even if my heart hadn't been behind the quick kiss I had shared with Artan, if Kane found out about it, he would be so, so hurt.

But how could I hide that from him? If I wanted a true and strong relationship with him, I couldn't hide the kiss.

A sudden urge to talk to Ellie hit me, but I was sure what she would say: to not tell Kane. She would argue that a kiss wasn't the same as sex. Trina had cheated on Kane by sleeping with another man, while I had allowed Artan to kiss me for a moment. Truth was, to me, a kiss could be as intimate as sex. And in some ways, a kiss was even more loving.

Kane deserved to know the truth, but I wasn't sure how to tell him about it.

I heard the crunching of boots and I instantly knew.

"Hey," Kane said, approaching me.

I kept my gaze on the moon's shine over the water's surface. "Hi."

"Won't you look at me?" The tone of his voice rubbed me wrong.

He knew. I didn't know how he had already found out, but I was sure he knew.

Slowly, I spun around and faced him.

Back straight, shoulders squared, Kane stood about three feet from me. His arms were crossed over his chest, and his brows were curled down—he was bracing himself.

By Saint Sara-la-Kali.

"I need to tell you something," I blurted, before I lost the nerve and never told him anything.

His chin dipped once. "I know."

My heart skipped a beat. So I was right. "How?"

He let out a string of curses. "So it's true. I didn't want to believe it, but I can see it in your face. It's true."

"How did you find out?"

"Your mother was worried you had gone alone after Artan, so she sent me to find you. When I got to his house, the door was unlocked and he was seated on the stairs, drunk and confused. I asked where you were, and the only thing he told me was that you two had—" Exhaling loudly, Kane ran a hand through his hair. "That you two had kissed. He actually told me you kissed him first. That you wanted it."

"That's not true!"

"But you did kiss him."

It wasn't a question. I could lie. I could tell him I didn't. He would believe me; I knew he would. But if somehow he ever found out the truth, it would only hurt more. "For a few seconds, yes."

His head dropped to his chest. Without another word, he spun around and began walking away.

I felt my heart wilting away. "Kane, wait." He paused, but didn't turn back. I wanted to go to him, to embrace him, to tell him it didn't mean anything, that he was the one I loved, and the one I would rather kiss, but the words got stuck in my throat. I bet Trina had said all those things to him when he caught her cheating. As far as I knew, she had fought for him afterward, and he wouldn't let her get close. A sob, sudden and violent, broke through my lips. "I'm sorry," I whispered. "I'm so sorry."

"Stop," he rasped. "I can't ... I need some time."

A second passed, a painful and long and heart-ripping

second, and then Kane dragged his feet away, like a defeated man.

Another sob rocked my core, and I fell seated on one of the rocks at the edge of the lake. How could I prove to him that the kiss hadn't meant anything? And why the hell did Artan lie about it? Out of spite? Because he was probably still drunk and hurt?

A tear rolled down my face.

Just when I thought things were finally working out, things were finally going my way, and we soon would find peace and live happily ever after, the world exploded. A friend died, her husband blamed me, and I ended up kissing someone else and hurting the man I loved.

Why, oh why, couldn't my life be a little bit simpler?

I wiped my face and stared at the shiny water surface. I blinked as Damara's and Trina's face appeared, just under the water. Had Kane already gone too far from me and the craziness was pushing back, hard and fast?

But there was no pain in my head, no other impossible images assaulting my mind.

I blinked again, and their faces were gone.

Despite all the shit going on in my personal life, I had to solve another problem before of all the problems in my love life. I had to find a way of defeating Damara—and taking Trina down along with her. They had to pay for all they had done.

Even if the cost of that was my life.

CONTINUE READING ABOUT MIRELLA'S ADVENTURES ON *WAR Maiden*, book 6 of The Fire Heart Chronicles.

THANK YOU

Thank you for reading *Fate Summoner*!

Reviews are very important for authors. If you liked my book, please consider leaving a review on your preferred online store and/or on goodreads, please!

Grab the next book in the series now:

War Maiden

Don't forget to sign up for my Newsletter to find out about new releases, cover reveals, giveaways, and more!

If you want to see exclusive teasers, help me decide on covers, read excerpts, talk about books, etc, join my reader group on Facebook: Juliana's Club!

Want to join my ARC team (Advanced Reading Copy)? Find out how by clicking here!

ABOUT THE AUTHOR

While USA Today Bestselling Author Juliana Haygert dreams of being Wonder Woman, Buffy, or a blood elf shadow priest, she settles for the less exciting—but equally gratifying—life as a wife, a mother, and an author. She resides in North Carolina and spends her days writing about kick-ass heroines and the heroes who drive them crazy.

Subscribe to her mailing list to receive emails of announcement, events, and other fun stuff related to her writing and her books: www.bit.ly/JuHNL

For more information:
www.julianahaygert.com

facebook.com/julianahaygert
twitter.com/juliana_haygert
instagram.com/juliana.haygert

ALSO BY JULIANA HAYGERT

www.julianahaygert.com/books/

Free

Into the Darkest Fire

Tested

Rite World: Blackthorn Hunters Academy

The Demon Kiss (Book 1)

The Hunter Secret (Book 2)

The Soul Bond (Book 3)

The Shadow Trials (Book 4)

The Infernal Curse (Book 5)

Rite World

The Vampire Heir (Book 1)

The Witch Queen (Book 2)

The Immortal Vow (Book 3)

The Warlock Lord (Book 4)

The Wolf Consort (Book 5)

The Crystal Rose (Book 6)

The Fire Heart Chronicles

Heart Seeker (Book 1)

Flame Caster (Book 2)

Sorrow Bringer (Book 3)

Earth Shaker (Novella)

Soul Wanderer (Book 4)

Fate Summoner (Book 5)

War Maiden (Book 6)

The Everlast Series

Destiny Gift (Book 1)

Soul Oath (Book 2)

Cup of Life (Book 3)

Everlasting Circle (Book 4)

Willow Harbor Series

Hunter's Revenge (Book 3)

Siren's Song (Book 5)